Willow's White House

Berma the Bench

D1252977

The Stray Club

"Nilsson's second book proves that this promising new author is no one-hit wonder. *The Land of the Strays* is a classic in the making that no childhood library should be without."

—Naomi Rougeau
Senior Fashion Features Editor, *ELLE*

"Our children face unprecedented headwinds in learning acceptance, empathy, and compassion today. The diversity of characters throughout *The Land of the Strays* gives the reader insight and perspective into many of these challenges, while providing a powerful ally against the ever-present influence of social media. Parents take comfort knowing Summer's book can be referenced for positive affirmations of the life and coping skills our children need to be taught."

—Michael Ziegler
Speedway Motorsports

"*The Land of the Strays* is a poignant story filled with incredible imagery which automatically encourages the reader to look within to see and hear the wondrous uniqueness and power inside themselves and each other. It is through listening that we learn to see things differently."

—Dr. Luci Higgins
Superintendent of Schools,
Cornerstone Christian Schools

"In her second book, *The Land of the Strays*, Summer Nilsson sets the stage for learning through a creative path and a natural course to embrace the challenges our nation's children will face. Underscored with a solid, values-based approach in the narrative, this book will be a seminal example for young and old alike, for it captures our imagination and helps chart a course for the future. *The Land of the Strays* is not about correcting . . . it is about connecting through themes of self-respect and dignity for all. A must-read for every bookshelf, especially for those who care about our nation's future, our young adults."

—Virgil "Duz" Packett
Major General, US Army (Ret), Apache Pilot

"*The Land of the Strays* teaches the importance of resilience and overcoming the inner voice of self-doubt to pursue one's dreams. Highly recommend for youth of all ages!"

—Professor Rockford Weitz
Director, Maritime Studies Program,
The Fletcher School, Tufts University

"Like her first book, *The Land of the Pines*, Summer Nilsson's *The Land of the Strays* is simultaneously magical and thoughtful. Grey the Kitten now lives in the city, a place of fascination, temptation, and, as the little cat discovers, cruel prejudice. Nilsson's characters are whimsical and make-believe; the moral choices they confront are not."

—Austin Bay
National Security Columnist and Author,
Cocktails from Hell: Five Wars Shaping the 21st Century

"With valuable lessons of kindness, friendship, and self-worth woven into rich storytelling and lush illustrations, the Loodor Tales Series is a delightful and timely encouragement for today's young readers."

—Julie Goff
Operation Kindness

"*The Land of the Strays* will appeal to readers of all ages—as will the uplifting message of acceptance. Indelible animal characters headline this winsome tale of fellowship and magic."

—Kirkus Indie Reviews

"Adventures abound in the *The Land of the Strays*, whose animal cast struggles to overcome their prejudices, learning to treat everyone with respect and compassion."

—Foreword Clarion Review

loodʊr tales

THE LAND
of the
STRAYS

SUMMER NILSSON

with New York Times Bestselling Illustrator Nancy Harrison

Loodor Tales: The Land of the Strays

Printed in the United States of America
10 9 8 7 6 5 4 3 2 1

Published by Loodor Publishing
Dallas, Texas

For more information or to contact the author,
please visit www.loodor.com.

Cover design, interior design, and composition by Loodor Publishing

Library of Congress Control Number: 2022903058

Publisher's Cataloging-in-Publication data is available.

Print ISBN: 978-1-954401-02-0
eBook ISBN: 978-1-954401-03-7

Distributed by Greenleaf Book Group

For ordering information, please contact Greenleaf Book Group at
PO Box 91869, Austin, TX 78709, 512.891.6100.

Dedicated to the military and frontline responders
Honoring the men, women, and animals
who serve our country every day

CONTENTS

PROLOGUE

S cout watched the snakes swarm as his teammates floated over the horizon.

Scout had trained for this day. He gave his team everything he had. In the end, he wasn't sure it mattered. Their path had been paved well before they arrived, and by a much higher power. Scout wore that newfound wisdom like a badge on his torn, battered vest.

Scout whispered to himself: "Today we saw life from the other side, and we realized there's always a reason. To search and to save, in salute we shall wave, and learn not to brand brethren of treason."

CHAPTER ONE

SADDLE UP

G rey the Kitten knew there would be no do-overs. This moment was do-or-die.

Grey ran like her life depended on it. The red ore dirt propelled her feet forward as the twigs under her toes bounced against the sun-scorched grass. Every muscle in her body was on high alert. Grey's attention rose from her paws to her legs to her ears, which were ringing. Grey could hear Biggie the Deer and Miss Jay the Bird screaming behind her.

"Hurry!" Miss Jay urged.

"Watch out!" Biggie begged.

"Run faster!" Miss Jay yelled.

"Jump NOW!" Biggie demanded.

Her friends' fear hung in the hot, thick air. As if on cue, the pine trees swayed back and forth. Their breeze carried a sense of urgency through the rumbling wind. In response, the frogs on the trail began to chant Grey's name. Their deep baritone voices shook the mountain like the beat of a ceremonial drum. Grey felt both terrified and triumphant. She hoped the two emotions had emerged at the same time for the purpose of guiding her to victory. She'd dreamt of this moment from the day she was born in the Jam Barn of Black Mountain Farm. BMF, as she called it.

BMF was the only home Grey had ever known. She knew how much she was leaving behind, and there were no guarantees that the grass would be any greener on the other side of this gate. Grey wasn't running for that reason. She was running because this was her destiny.

Grey had been born a barn cat. Nothing more, and nothing less. Until yesterday. Yesterday, everything changed. While visiting Bo the Wise Owl at Lone Star

Lodge, Grey discovered she had a magical voice. Her words held the power to take any shape she directed as long as she used them for good. Her voice could build things or break them. Today, it would break them. Grey knew it was the only way she would survive.

"Break it!" Grey shouted.

Grey watched her words take flight. The words molded to make a perfect circle before speeding ahead to furiously whip through a wooden fence a few yards away. Grey saw the circle of words cut through the center of the fence before disappearing into a cloud of wooden dust. Grey followed her voice with the perfect form of a barn cat emboldened with purpose. She jumped carefully through the newly created hole. She felt the raw edge of the reshaped fence as it dared her to shift so much as a centimeter in either direction. She held her breath, tucked her head, straightened her legs, and pointed her toes. Grey's tail cleared the final stretch of gate just as her life flashed before her.

Grey landed squarely in front of a dark, black sedan on the other side of the fence. But as fate would have it, today was not Grey's day to die.

. . . .

Grey had been on a mission to meet her human. She'd hoped to ride off into the sunset together. Little did Grey know, she'd already spent the week with her mom-to-be. Grey recognized the woman as soon as she stepped out of the black car. Grey couldn't have been more excited to learn that her new mom was Anne, Miss B's niece.

Miss B and Mr. Joe owned BMF. Anne was born and raised in the city, but she'd spent every spring break at Black Mountain Farm. As Anne got older, she returned for stays in the summer, too. Grey heard that Anne felt more at home on the farm than in the city.

Anne had long brown hair and soft green eyes that blended with the blades of grass. Grey could tell Anne was totally confident in who she was. Anne also had a style that separated her from the rest of the small town. She wore long, flowy dresses that blew in the breeze to reveal rugged, worn work boots. She was a contradiction of terms: both delicate and tough, simple and bold.

Anne had a reputation for knowing the mountain better than the animals. Grey had heard stories about Anne's driving, in particular. Anne was famous for zooming by the barn in a four-wheeler named "Miss Mule." Miss Mule had a hot-pink seat cover, on which Anne had written the words *Dare Me*. Grey knew it was considered normal to find Anne covered in mud and smiling from ear to ear at the end of the day. Anne parked Miss Mule directly in front of the Jam Barn for all the animals to see.

Grey had a hunch that Miss Mule didn't mind getting dirty. In fact, Miss Mule seemed to wear the mud like a cloak of character. Her wheels squealed with steadfast determination on the slippery trails. The animals had all learned to hide when they heard Miss Mule's motor crank. Grey suddenly wondered if Anne was any more careful when driving a car.

Grey knew the ball was in her court, so she pranced over to Anne and leaned against her leg. Grey guessed it was the right move because Anne promptly picked her up and placed her on a blanket on the front seat. Grey tried to keep her eyes open, but the magnitude of the moment hit her all at once. She couldn't remember a time when she hadn't wished for this very outcome. She allowed herself to drift into the dream of her day.

From time to time, Grey woke long enough to look outside. She noticed that the road signs seemed much larger than the trail markers on the mountain. Grey couldn't have been happier to ride and rest . . . while it lasted. Then Anne began to talk, a lot. Only Anne wasn't speaking to Grey. At least, not at first.

"Aunt B, I did something," Anne began. "I hope you're OK with it, but it's too late if you're not. I took the cat . . . yep, that gray kitten. The one I kept bugging you about. Remember how I told you to bring it in the house? Well, if I hadn't seen it firsthand, I would swear this wasn't possible: I watched that kitten jump THROUGH the gate. Not over it—through it.

"Just as I was pulling out, she landed directly in front of my car. I didn't hit her, but I'm heading straight to the vet to make sure she's OK. She doesn't seem frightened at all. Yes, Stan might kill me. No, I don't know how Blaze and Lane will react. I can't worry about that."

Grey listened intently. She tried to make sense of the one-sided conversation. Stan might kill Anne, and no one knew what Blaze and Lane would do.

Great start, Grey noted to herself.

Grey's gut told her that the bigger issue was the vet. However, Grey couldn't focus because Anne was speaking again. Grey noticed that this time, Anne was staring at her as she spoke.

"I promise to take care of you," Anne said. "From this moment on, we're in this together. The first stop will be the vet. It won't be your favorite place, but it's necessary. The vet will clean you up. I'll be with you the whole time."

Grey saw Anne fiddle with the keys. It was only then that Grey noticed the car had stopped. Grey watched as Anne wrapped the blanket around her body. She had no time to get her bearings. Grey knew there was no way out of whatever was happening next. She was trapped.

Grey noticed the smell first. It smelled like the cleaning supplies Miss B kept in the back of the barn. Grey heard dogs barking in the background, but she was blinded by a sudden light. Then, out of nowhere, Grey felt a deep sting in her leg.

Seriously? Grey screamed to herself. *What in the actual . . . ?*

Grey lost her train of thought when her eyesight returned to reveal a blue, foamy bucket.

Surely not, Grey silently mused.

Grey held her breath and closed her eyes. If the vet was going to drown her, so be it. She tried, and failed, to hold her nose. Everything else went by in a blur.

Grey had dreamt about her new life. Life with her human. She'd imagined what her soft bed would feel like. Grey felt certain the universe was having a large laugh at her expense as the day detoured away from the glowing house she'd seen in her dreams. Anne, on the other hand, seemed to be thrilled with the outcome. Anne was all smiles. *She* hadn't just survived the dirty dunk.

Grey was too tired to fight. She allowed Anne to carry her back to the car. In spite of it all, Grey had to admit that she felt like a fresh city cat . . . and she liked it. Her nails were trimmed. Her fur was slicked back. She'd even scored a new necklace. It was gray and black with a pink rose pattern. Anne called it a collar. The collar had a round, gold charm that dangled against Grey's bright, white chest.

Grey hoped this was the start to her charmed life after all. She was done holding her breath.

. . . .

Grey couldn't believe her eyes when Anne finally parked in front of their home. It was just before sunset. The high-rise was built with an orange shade of brick; it was the same soft color as the ore rock on the farm trails at BMF. It felt as though someone had pulled pieces from Grey's past to provide the foundation for her future. The building seemed to glow all the way to the sky. Even the glass on the front door reflected the golden hour light of the day.

Grey noticed a bronze statue of a dog as they entered the building. The word *Argos* was etched into the base of the statue. Grey wondered who the dog was and what the statue stood for. Anne carried Grey from the car to the lobby, and from the lobby to a tiny room with beeping buttons. Anne called it the elevator. The buttons talked over themselves. Grey could tell they were excited to greet the new resident cat. They glowed like the building. From the elevator, Anne walked to a brown door. Grey was suddenly very grateful to her new mom for the slam dunk of a pit stop that had made her presentable.

Anne opened the door. Grey gasped. She felt every hair on her shiny body stand up. Stan the Man, Lane the Labrador, and Blaze the Bengal were all waiting inside the door. Time stood still as each side sized up the other. Stan appeared to be calming his crew and insisting that they welcome their new roommate.

Grey felt herself reverting back to a barn cat filled with uncertainty. Old insecurities sounded like an alarm in her head. Grey worried if she'd somehow failed when Blaze turned and walked away, offering no greeting. No "Hi-ya, partner." More of an "Eh, can't be bothered with the barn cat." At least, that's how Grey heard the conversation play out in her mind.

Lane, on the other hand, was all love. Anne placed Grey on the floor. This prompted sloppy, wet licks and next-level enthusiasm from the sweet Lab. Grey saw that Lane had tender eyes and a huge, heartfelt smile. Grey noticed that Lane was also wearing a collar. Lane's collar was a thick brown leather with a silver buckle, and stars that went all the way around his neck. Grey noted that Lane's collar matched Stan's brown cowboy boots.

Maybe Lane needs a friend, too, Grey hoped to herself. Either way, she appreciated the affection. She needed reassurance from a roommate. Grey felt like she was entering into a lion's den.

"Saddle up, country girl!" Lane laughed. "And don't bother with the Bengal. I call her Blaze of Glory. She lives in her own world. Consider it a compliment that she didn't waste your time with false friendship. My advice: You be you. Authenticity always wins. Also, don't let anyone get in your head. If there's one thing I've learned, city cats can't combat sincerity."

Authenticity always wins.

Chapter Two

The Listening Lab

Lane was born to Janis, and Janis was a local treasure. In her prime, Janis had been the fastest dog in the county. Janis belonged to Lloyd, a rancher and an "old-school" charmer. Lloyd could tap his cowboy hat and grin with the best of them.

Lloyd's happiest days were spent riding around in his pickup truck. Janis always rode shotgun. Lloyd often joked that Janis drove his decisions, as well as his truck. Janis was Lloyd's leading lady. Lloyd believed that a man's choice of dog spoke to the man's character.

Lloyd was very protective of Janis's litters. Lloyd personally picked the right person for the right puppy, and he took pride in making the match. Lane noticed that Lloyd had been talking about his friend Stan for weeks. Lloyd and Stan had grown up together, and they were more like brothers than buddies.

Lane learned that Lloyd had given Stan the "first choice" of this litter. The dogs had all wondered which match would be made. Lane peeked around the corner as Stan pulled up. He, too, drove a truck. Stan jumped out of the truck wearing a baseball cap, a collared shirt, faded jeans, and cowboy boots that looked to be as old as the man wearing them.

Lane could immediately tell that Stan was every dog's dream. He looked rugged but refined in an effortlessly cool kind of way. Stan walked with a swagger. Lane and his siblings listened closely as the two friends caught up.

"Are you ever going to replace that old truck?" Lloyd said with a smirk.

"Shelby?" Stan laughed. "Absolutely not." He feigned shock that Lloyd could even suggest such a thing. "Shelby drives herself these days. I sit back and let her lead the way. Besides, Shelby also drives my mother crazy. That's reason enough to keep her around."

"How is your mom, by the way?" Lloyd carefully inquired.

"Nothing new to report," Stan confirmed. "Mom's great, so long as it's all on her terms. I don't know how Dad does it. Well, yeah, I do. He works all the time. The folks don't know I'm here, by the way. This will be my dog. Just mine."

"Got it," Lloyd said, smiling. "All families have their thing. Don't start thinking you're special just because yours is particularly high maintenance." Lloyd motioned toward the back of the house. "Follow me. The dogs are on the porch."

The five puppies panted as the men's footsteps approached. Lane knew that his brothers and sisters had all heard the banter, but only Lane could hear the rest. Lane could hear Stan's fear. Lane knew Stan's story before he knew Stan the Man.

. . . .

Lane was the middle pup in every way. Lane had two older brothers, Jake and John. They were bigger, stronger, and a light shade of yellow. He also had two younger sisters, Ally and Amy. They were smaller, smarter, and a dark shade of black. Lane was midsized and hands down the friendliest of the bunch. He was also the only one covered in velvety, chocolate-colored fur. His rich chocolate coloring was even more noticeable in contrast to his striking hazel eyes. The combination made him quite the catch.

Lane's siblings teased him in those first few months. They thought of every possible nickname, but "Sundae" was their favorite.

"What sounds good, Jake?" John asked every evening. "A chocolate sundae?"

Jake smiled.

The brothers bounced over to Lane. They wrestled and rolled around in the yard until one of them finally wore out. Lane found it both endearing and exhausting. He was sad to see John and Jake drop the roughhousing. That was the day they noticed that Lane was different.

Lane hadn't wanted to acknowledge it. He certainly didn't want to talk about it. For instance, his left ear felt strange. It didn't hurt. It flopped over and kind of buzzed from time to time. When it *zinged*, Lane would scratch it as hard as he could to make it flip back. Jake and John freaked out when Lane started shaking his head.

Lane told them he was trying to silence the sounds in his head. The explanation did not go over well.

Lane knew he was hearing voices. At first, he actually thought they were ghosts. Then, one day, it finally made sense . . . at least to him. Lane had dozed off while lying on the porch. He was miles into a dream when a sound drew him back into the real world.

"Who are you kidding?" the voice emerged. "Nobody wants the smallest one. It's called the runt for a reason."

Lane raised his head and looked around. John and Jake were playing in the sprinkler system. Ally was fast asleep in the shade. That's when Lane noticed Amy staring off into space. She was nestled underneath the trees in the backyard. Lane slowly walked over to his youngest sister's side.

"Mind if I sit?" Lane asked. Lane was careful to acknowledge that Amy was clearly having a moment. Amy nodded and wiped her face as she motioned for Lane to join. Lane knew he was going out on a limb. A long limb, for that matter. Lane figured that if he was wrong, there was no harm in what he was about to say. He just had to be careful not to scare his sister.

"I was thinking about something," Lane began. "You're clearly the smallest one now. That's all about to change. You're going to outgrow the rest of us. It's obvious by your paws. So, when you do, I want you to promise that you'll do me a favor. Take those two idiots down." Lane pointed to their brothers. Jake and John were still rolling around.

Lane looked to Amy for a sign, any sign. He noticed that his sister's face had begun to soften. Lane watched as Amy looked around to see if someone was playing a prank on her. Lane guessed that Amy was trying to figure out how this conversation could have possibly transpired.

"Talk about timing," Amy finally replied. "It's like you just read my mind. Be careful, you don't want to get caged in there."

"No, I don't," Lane said, laughing. "It's just the dog days of summer, sis. I think we all have moments when we feel smaller than we actually are. Big things are going to happen for each of us when the time is right. You gotta have faith."

Lane had forced himself to remain in the moment. He pretended to share in the sheer luck of his timing. He then turned to stare into the distance—the same distance his sister had just occupied. Lane sat very still while his mind raced. He had just heard the sound of his sister's inner thoughts. He'd *heard* her thoughts. Thoughts she didn't actually say out loud.

Lane sat in silence and wondered who, or what else, he could hear.

. . . .

Lane thought back to his first memories in the house. It had been a bittersweet day when he left his brothers and sisters behind. Lane had ridden shotgun in Shelby's old front seat and smiled the whole way. Stan lived on the top floor of the building, and Lane quickly discovered that their unit wrapped around the entire west wing.

Back then, the house had been a gigantic bachelor pad, perfect for a guy's guy and his growing Lab. The furniture had been handed down by Stan's parents and included an oversized sofa, two torn and comfy chairs, and an old, stained rug that shed as much as Lane.

Stan and Lane lived like kings. From Monday through Friday, they overlooked the city from their west-facing nest. Then, on the weekends, they drove out to Stan's ranch. Stan let Lane loose to chase the squirrels from tree to tree.

How times have changed, Lane thought to himself with a laugh.

First came Blaze. No one had seen that coming. Lane would never forget Stan's compassion in embracing Blaze in all of her glory.

"Your father has finally agreed to retire," Jules announced during an unscheduled visit. "You know I've been pushing this for years. We'll be spending a lot more time traveling. We want to be able to pick up and go whenever we like. Your father worked hard for this. He's earned it."

"Let me get this straight," Stan said. He stared in disbelief. "Dad's retiring. So you want to leave your cat with me? Is this a joke?"

Lane could tell that Stan was getting emotional. His mother, Jules, was not.

"You were on a waiting list for two years to get this cat," Stan continued. "It's all you talked about. It had to be *this* cat. You treat her like a prized possession. You can't just drop an animal off at someone else's house. It doesn't work that way. You made a commitment."

"You're not someone else," Jules countered, her voice raised. "You're my son and leaving Blaze behind will be a gift for both of you. Blaze needs to have someone around to greet her at the end of each day. I can't do it anymore. And let's be honest, you need something feminine in this house."

"Mom, this has nothing to do with me," Stan said with a sigh. "Or my house." He paused to take a deep breath before turning to face Lane.

"Buddy, I'm going to need your help," Stan began. "This is going to be a tough transition for that cat. I know it's been just us boys for a while. No matter what Blaze does, give her a chance. She deserves to have a loving home too."

Lane studied the high-brow Bengal and her brown box of possessions. He noted that Blaze was wearing a rhinestone collar with a name tag. Naturally. Lane licked Stan's face and took the request to heart.

In the following months, Lane tried everything he could to make Blaze comfortable. He brought her his bone and his stuffed duck. When that didn't work, he gave Blaze his blanket. She wanted none of it. Blaze turned up her nose at everything except Stan. Blaze followed Stan into every room and never left his side. Lane wondered sadly whether Blaze was scared to be left alone or left behind. He looked and listened for any way he could help.

It had taken time, but the trio had finally found their routine as a blended family. Then Stan met Anne. It wasn't long before Anne moved in. The sofa, chairs, and rug in the living room were all quickly replaced.

Anne redecorated with shiny furniture that no one was allowed to use. To this day, Lane couldn't understand how that made any sense.

And here we are, Lane thought to himself. *A party of five.*

Lane was glad to have Grey in the house. He connected with her immediately. Lane bet Grey would have liked the old furniture better too.

CHAPTER THREE

CONCRETE CHAOS

G rey walked through every room of her new home. Anne followed closely behind.

A brown wooden table occupied the entry-way. On the table sat a stack of books with a bowl to one side and a small square plate on the other. Grey noticed that the square plate had been painted to resemble a red bull's-eye. Anne had dropped her keys on the center of the plate. A large black-and-white picture of a cowboy wearing chaps hung above the table. A light pointed to the picture. Grey guessed the picture was important. She could see that someone had written the name *Wilson* in the far-right corner.

Grey walked from the entryway to the living room. She wasn't sure where to look first.

There were two floor-to-ceiling windows, each decorated with white fabric that hung neatly on both sides. The fabric frowned at Grey.

A long blue sofa and four chairs filled the space. Two of the chairs were cream-colored, and the other two were black. Grey noticed that the furniture looked relatively new. In contrast to the dusty barn she left behind, this room had no dirt, scratches, or scuffs of any kind. Grey faced the chairs and sofa in silence until one of them finally broke into laughter.

"We see you checking each of us out," the cream-colored chair by the window said. "Blue's your new best friend. Jump all over him. He loves it, but we're off-limits. Anne doesn't allow anyone to actually sit on us. And for your own sake, think twice before climbing the curtains. Your vanity may vault you up, but it's a false sense of footing when you climb over someone to reach the top. You'll see the same faces on the same drapes all the way back down."

"Let me guess," Grey said, smirking at the glass table sitting between the four chairs. "You're just there to look pretty too?"

"That depends on whether or not you want to stay a while." The glass table grinned. "Blaze gets in trouble every day. And Lane's tail . . . don't even get me started on what a disaster that is. Lane's a bull in a china shop. He runs around in circles."

Doesn't everyone? Grey thought to herself as she moved from the living room to a hallway. There, Grey stopped in her tracks. The hallway was filled with farm animals. Not real ones, of course. Anne had taken photographs of the summers she spent at Black Mountain Farm. The pictures were hung in two horizontal rows that lined the entire wall. Frogs and birds, flowers and trees, even the goats made an appearance. It looked to Grey as though a baby goat had literally walked right up to Anne's camera. Grey realized that she was surrounded by friends, old and new. She felt more at home by the minute.

The hallway led Grey into the bedroom. Grey noticed a fresh blanket on the left side of the bed and instinctively knew it was her spot to sleep. Grey saw that Lane was already sitting in his dog bed by the window. Lane looked exhausted. Grey jumped onto the bed and looked out the window to face her new world. A world of concrete chaos.

Grey watched as a neon glow outlined the buildings, tracing the city like a sketchpad. She then studied the boxes hanging over the streets below. The boxes blinked with red, yellow, and green lights. The lights marked the movement on the paved roads. They seemed to control the cars. Grey wondered who controlled the lights. She looked to the sky and imagined the moon and the stars sitting atop the tallest building, watching as the crowds and the cars followed their every command.

Grey nestled on her new blanket, curious as to who really pushed the buttons around here.

4

CHAPTER FOUR

STARBOARD

Polaris the North Star, known as "Polly" to her partners, listened as her team of stars shared ideas for the very large task at hand. Polly had spent the past three hours presenting her plan. Each and every detail had to be perfect. The plan needed to be precise. Polly had even considered the delays that could be caused by a dog's free will to chase its tail in lieu of its dreams.

To each their own, Polly thought, *but this dog must remain focused.*

Polly had made a promise. She had guaranteed the dog's safety and success. Polly very rarely made a promise of such magnitude, but she had a track record for consistency. Polly had overextended her reach to assure the dog's grandmother that she could deliver the dog to its destiny. Polly understood that she would have to wish upon her fellow stars to honor her word.

Polly was a straight shooter. She knew she wasn't the brightest star in the sky. However, she was a leader. All of the other stars circled around her. Polly was their fixed point. The entire sky, and its ability to guide animals, was based on her stability. Polly took this responsibility seriously, and she was a force to be reckoned with. A force . . . with a twinkle in her eyes. Polly's eyes revealed a sense of humor, which her fellow stars knew she appreciated above all else.

"Look, I know this entire operation circles around *me,*" Polly pronounced. "I represent due north, otherwise known as true self. Animals look for me when they need to validate a feeling as a fact. But my success depends on your success. That's the beauty of our system. I'd like to go around the table and review each group's role. We can't afford any mistakes where this dog is concerned; he represents too much in the big picture.

"Pherkad and Kochab, can we start with you?"

"My friends call me Gamma," Pherkad offered. "As you all know, we're the official Guardians of the North Star. Since the North Star represents true self, this means that our role is to safeguard identity. The short answer is that we're here to protect Polly. By watching over Polly, we protect the many animals that will rise to greatness as a result of her guidance."

"You're making this way too complicated," Kochab interrupted. "First, I go by Beta, because they 'beta stay outta my way.'"

The group giggled. Beta was all brawn.

"I don't have Gamma's soft touch, so I'll cut straight to the chase," Beta continued. "We're the offensive line. If we think an animal has bad intentions, we'll block them. It's our job to make sure no animal reaches this dog unless he or she genuinely wants to see it succeed. We'll use whatever force is necessary."

"Got it," Polly acknowledged, clearly grateful for her guardians. "Merak and Dubhe, what about you?"

"As the official Pointers of the Stars, Dubhe and I always take a very hands-on approach," Merak said with a smile. "Our job is to make sure the dog sees signs along the way. We're here to assure him that he's on the right path. We will point out the obvious, but we'll also offer a subtle nod in the right direction when he needs a gentle nudge."

"Perfect," Polly applauded. Polly loved the Pointers' creativity and couldn't wait to see what signs the duo came up with for this dog. "Mizar and Alcor, what about you guys?"

"Doubt Detectors, at your service," Mizar replied. "Call us Mi and Co."

Polly smiled as Mi and Co stood together to emphasize their collaborative position. Polly watched the two stars move together as one. It took a trained eye to catch that Mi was the more dominant star and separate entity.

"We know every animal has a voice in its head," Mi offered. "The voice that's always a second behind their goals and racing to take control. That voice is called doubt. Doubt is an imposter. Animals have to focus really hard to see that doubt isn't actually attached to them. Doubt only exists to occupy space in our minds and diminish our light. It makes animals feel afraid. Our job will be to identify doubt and do everything we can to keep it away from this dog."

"Everyone needs doubt detectors," Polly determined. "Alioth, talk us through your part."

"I'm the Keeper of Joy," Alioth said, beaming. "Call me Ali for short. I've been around for a while. I shine the brightest among this group. My job will be to help the dog discover what makes him happy by spotlighting his moments of joy."

Polly had always been in awe of Ali. Polly stared at Ali's rosy pink cheeks and huge smile. Ali's smile reflected her eternal hope for a happy world.

"I feel confident that everyone here will do their part," Polly confirmed. She pulled at the sleeves of her jacket and offered one last suggestion.

"We'll all bear the weight of this burden if anything goes wrong. This dog will find magic in his moment of need. Let's send a strong message that the sky's the limit when we work together. Part of how we present ourselves is dressing the part. Can I count on each of you to wear a star suit?"

"I'll wear it, but I won't like it," Beta objected. "I do agree, though. If we're a team, we should appear unified across all fronts."

"On that note," Polly concluded, "let's meet at Cloud Nine before the big finale."

. . . .

Polly suggested that Gamma and Beta stay behind so they could speak privately about their next steps.

"Gamma, why don't you start?" Polly suggested.

"I get that we all approach things differently, but I'd like for Beta and me to be on the same page where this dog is concerned," Gamma said delicately.

"I intend to knock down anything that gets near him," Beta stated. "I made that clear."

"I just don't think that's the right page." Gamma sighed. "I know this sounds risky, but I think we need to pull back just a little. There are two ways to handle confrontation. Some are fast to react. They say the first thing that comes to their mind."

"They say what *needs* to be said so others can move on to the next task," Beta clarified. "They get the job done."

"Yep, and that approach can be effective," Gamma acknowledged. "But this dog doesn't need any more training on how to react quickly. He's got that down. He has to learn the art of winning in silence. I think the fight he's having with himself is far more danger-ous than with any animal on his path."

"What are you saying?" Beta asked, frowning.

"This dog will solve every problem and search behind every door before he stops to answer the single question that stands in his way."

"What's the question?" Beta asked.

"Am I enough?" Gamma stated.

"You think the stars can help him reach that kind of clarity?" Beta questioned.

"Yes, we can," Gamma said, smiling as she gazed at Polly. "However, we can't block an animal from an internal battle. That's the one line we can't cross. The stars can provide signs and dissolve doubt. We can safeguard the journey and highlight happiness to ensure that joy isn't taken for granted. But when it's all said and done, we're just here to guide the ship. The dog has to win the war."

*Doubt is an
imposter.*

CHAPTER FIVE

THE STRAY CLUB

G rey awakened to find the sun waving through the window. Grey stretched and realized she was starving. She'd been too overwhelmed to eat the night before. She heard voices and followed the sounds into the next room, grateful to see Lane standing by. Grey knew that Lane would fill her in on what to do next.

"Sleep OK?" Lane asked, greeting her with a grin. "Listen, I wanted to talk to you about the schedule for the morning. It's the same thing every day. You'll get the hang of it."

Grey listened as she passed Lane. Six silver bowls were lined up in a row. Grey noted that the two bowls on the far-right side were considerably bigger. They obviously belonged to Lane. The other four bowls were anyone's guess. Grey wished she knew the rules for this kind of thing. She was certain that house cats had their own system. Unfortunately, Grey didn't know anything about it.

"Oh, I bet they didn't have bowls in the *barn*," Blaze said with a smirk. "This must be so confusing. Don't worry, I'm here to help. Think of me as the counselor of your charm school. I'll be your source for all answers related to etiquette. *Etiquette* is just a fancy word for 'socially acceptable behavior.'

"Let's start with the bowls: Always start on the outside and work your way in. Meaning, *your* food and water bowls are on the far left, mine are in the middle, and Lane's are on the far right. The bowls are lined up in the order that we arrived here. We go by seniority."

Grey heard Blaze's tone and didn't appreciate it. Still, Grey was hungry and grateful to know which bowls belonged to her. The moment Grey tasted the food, Blaze became background noise, anyway. Grey licked the bowl dry. She could tell from Blaze's stare that bowl-licking didn't pass for socially acceptable behavior.

"You'll fit right in," Blaze snarled at Grey's gaffe.

Grey heard Lane clear his throat.

"Anne's going to be here in about two minutes," Lane warned. "Every morning, she gets up and feeds us first. Then she gets dressed to take us for our morning walk on the Trinity Trails. For our walk, I'll be on a leash. You and Blaze will probably ride together in the s-t-r-o-l-l-e-r."

Grey caught the change in Lane's voice as he completed the last sentence. Particularly, the last word. Grey assumed that Lane's voice had risen a few octaves in a failed attempt to actually stop the words from coming out at all. Grey watched Lane's eyes move from her to Blaze and back.

Grey understood. It didn't take a rocket scientist to figure out that Blaze probably hadn't shared anything before. Grey didn't have time to think about it. Just as Lane predicted, Anne raced into the room. Anne walked straight over to Grey and grabbed her up in an upside-down, airborne hug. Grey heard her collar rattle as Anne squeezed her within an inch of her life.

Lane laughed, but Grey noticed that Blaze had a funny look on her face. Grey wondered why a suffocating spiral spin would bother Blaze. Grey made a mental note to ask Lane about it after their morning walk.

Grey saw Anne motion toward a stroller made with mesh, see-through sides. She guessed the panels provided the passengers with a view. Grey watched Blaze jump in first, quickly claiming her spot on the right side. Careful not to go astray, Grey understood that seniority, and status, remained on the right side of the stroller.

. . . .

Grey was immediately struck by the sound. Noises from every direction. Horns honking. Dogs barking. Tires screeching. Trees blowing. Music blaring. Grey didn't know where to focus first.

"How does anyone concentrate in the city?" Grey asked.

"For now, just watch as we go," Lane replied. "We'll walk a quarter of a mile along this tree-lined sidewalk. Pay close attention to the neighborhood shops along the way. On the left, you'll see Canines & Coffee. It's a combination dog park and coffeehouse. People stop there if they don't want to go all the way to the trails. There's no shortage of blond Labs and tall lattes in there, but, personally, I prefer the tails on the trails.

"On the right, you'll see The Dry Bark. It has a yellow paw print on the glass next to the front door. The Argos dogs go to The Dry Bark to get groomed. You may have stopped there on your way from the farm. I can't speak to the feline side of things, but for dogs, it's the best blowout in town. You get a massage, too. I leave that place feeling like a million bucks.

"Next, we have The Rose Garden. It's the neighborhood flower shop. Stan's a regular, so I'm there a lot. Once we pass The Rose Garden, we'll reach the gate to enter the Trinity Trails. You can't miss it."

"Is it always this busy?" Grey grilled Lane.

"This is nothing," Lane said with a laugh. "Wait for the weekends."

Grey was about to reply when she saw the entrance for the first time. Two stone pillars were nestled side by side, connecting an open black iron gate with the words *Trinity Trails* spelled out in a horizontal line. To the left of the gate sat a red caboose with "No. 708" painted in white on its side. Grey noticed that the caboose had clearly been restored to its original glory. On the right side of the gate, Grey isolated the source of music: the Trinity Trails Roundhouse. The Roundhouse appeared to be a gathering spot with chairs and tables positioned in a large circle. Barn lights hung in the trees that lined the walkway to a red brick building covered with old signs.

"I know . . . it's a lot." Lane chuckled. "Let's start with the gate. This is the entrance for bicyclists, runners, skateboarders, and walkers. We all share the same five-mile path, but the skaters march to a totally different drum.

"The Trinity Trails were built on top of old railroad tracks. Hence, the caboose. It's the actual caboose that was used to service the tracks. The railroad and caboose were abandoned a long time ago. That's when the land was purchased by a man named Warren Whistler. Warren created walking trails where the railroads once ran. It ended up being Warren's legacy. He devoted his final days to walking the trails.

"Warren kept a whistle in his pocket. It was a gift from his wife. He blew the whistle every evening at sunset. It was Warren's way of expressing gratitude for the land, the light, and the opportunity of the day. Warren's wife listened for the sound as a sign that he was on his way home.

"When Warren died, he donated the land to the city on the condition that the trails be made available to everyone. It was Warren's way of giving back. He transitioned his private property to public gain. The only requirement was that a park be built by the large creek along the trails. Warren insisted that the park include a fountain for dogs to drink. The city named it Whistler Park. The dogs call it the 'water cooler.'"

Grey studied the fountain ahead. It sat in the center of a concrete overpass that connected the trails to the creek. At first glance, the overpass appeared to be floating. It took Grey a few seconds to realize that it was sitting on stilts and designed to overlook the grassy lawn that backed right up to the water.

"As you can imagine, Whistler Park is a home run for the city," Lane continued. "Over the years, they've added volleyball nets, restaurants, you name it. On weekends, locals enjoy picnics and parties, and they always leave scraps. Now, give me a sec."

Grey watched Lane line up at the water cooler. She then realized the dogs all knew one another. Grey was suddenly struck by how much she missed her farm family and friends. Grey looked on as Lane strutted back toward the stroller.

"I need you to pay close attention to me for a second," Lane requested. "The animals with leashes all understand that the trails are sacred ground. However, you'll also see lots of animals without leashes. They're waiting in the weeds. They belong to a much different breed: the Stray Club.

"The first rule among the 'leashes' is that you never talk about the Stray Club. The Stray Club represents what could happen on your worst day. Many of the strays have been separated from their former families. Some have never had a home at all. Either way, the strays are bold and direct, and they aren't afraid of anyone.

"The leashed community has also agreed not to look at members of the Stray Club. As a group, we avoid all eye contact. Speaking to the Stray Club is also frowned upon for everyone's safety. In short, we've all agreed never to talk to, or about, the Stray Club at all. I'm breaking the code today because you need to know the rules. Is that clear?"

"That's not clear at all!" Grey said with a gasp. "Do you not get that I came from a family of feral cats? My mother, brother, and sister ALL live in the wild. They see and accept me for who I am, and vice versa. It sounds to me like the strays are just like us. They simply chose a different life."

"Wrong," Lane insisted. "These animals are not the same as your mother, brother, and sister. It's important that you not make that mistake. The trail strays didn't choose this life. Many of them are here because they have no other place to go. Maybe their humans moved away. Maybe they were born here. Either way, they are dangerous. The strays will lie, cheat, and steal to save themselves."

"I don't believe that!" Grey retorted.

"You may have grown up in a barn, but you've never had to fight for your food," Lane explained. "It's life-changing to see strays for the first time. I get that. But it doesn't change the facts. The Stray Club can't be trusted, and we can't engage with them."

"Are you seriously trying to tell me who I can and can't talk to?" Grey balked. "I won't agree to that stupid rule. I can't! There must be something we can do to help these animals."

"We aren't in a position to help," Lane replied. "I know you would if you could. I would too. Unfortunately, it doesn't work that way. The Trinity Trails have a team that scatters food, but hunger feeds desperation. Most of these animals would do anything to be in our situation. They would be happy to live in the barn. They would give anything for the spot *you* left behind. The animals out here don't see you as a friend. They see you as someone that was given the life they wanted. Twice."

"Maybe that's true, but the point is that they see me," Grey concluded. "They see you too. You'd know that if you bothered to look beyond your leash. Living in a high-rise shouldn't elevate you to a high horse."

CHAPTER SIX

THE NAMESAKE

D avy the Domestic Shorthair was sleeping when he felt the floor shake. His left foot slipped out from under him. Davy had razor-sharp reflexes. He never lost his footing.

Davy's ears pinched down. He listened for a cue from the creek on which his home was built. Under ordinary circumstances, the creek kept him informed. However, these weren't ordinary circumstances.

The creek was under construction as the city worked to update the drainage system. Davy's house happened to sit beside a pipe that was key to the process. Davy had watched for months, learning about materials, installation, and engineering. Davy studied the crews of men as they molded metal and moved timber to reconstruct the creek's current. Davy kept track of the scraps and wondered why some materials were so easy to discard.

Davy saw the floor split. He watched as the crack raced and ripped their house from the last connecting piece of pipe. He screamed at his siblings to wake up. They scampered together before floating away in different directions. There had been no time for good-byes. Davy saw his entire life sink while he swam to survive. He'd kicked his arms and legs as fast as they would move. He gulped for air and strained his eyes in search of a safe spot to land. A house on a hill stood out from everything else on the horizon. It looked like a white box.

Davy grabbed at sticks and leaves. He held on to anything that would help him stay afloat. He flowed with the current and slowly inched closer to the other side. He could see the big, bright home that backed up to the creek. It looked clean and dry. He was neither.

He willed himself out of the water and took a moment to catch his breath.

Davy passed a bench and an old live oak tree. The bench winked as he walked by. Davy found it curious that the bench appeared to have been waiting for him. Davy noticed that the bench had a brass badge on its backside, but he didn't stop to read it. He simply didn't have time. The live oak branches blew a breeze that gently nudged Davy along. The breeze also carried the sweet smell of the freshly cut grass, which provided a soft cushion under Davy's tired paws. Davy's legs began to shake. His mouth was dry, and his eyes stung. Each step was a struggle as his body begged him to stop and rest. Davy couldn't quit. He had one goal: to make it inside that house.

Davy saw the front door of the big house swing open. He watched as a pair of brown braided leather sandals stepped onto the porch. Davy made it to the doormat before his body finally collapsed. He had nothing left to give.

"Hi, Davy," said the sandal-wearing woman as she smiled and knelt down to greet her defeated guest.

. . . .

Davy woke and wondered if it had all been a dream. He lifted his head and tried to stand. His arms and legs were pinned down. His heart began to race. What had happened to him?

Davy focused. She had called herself Willow, and him Davy. He remembered. Willow had picked him up and carried him to this very room. She'd wrapped his body in a towel and placed him on the sofa to sleep.

Davy turned his groggy head to survey his surroundings. The oval-shaped room was filled with warm sunlight, which beamed in from the glass windows. The windows revealed a garden and a clear view of the creek he'd left behind. Davy then noticed a white brick wall with a fireplace. Three jars of different colored sand sat on the left side of the mantle: one black, one tan, and one pink. The jars were each labeled with a location. A large black-and-white portrait of a couple had been placed on the right side of the mantle.

"Don't worry," Willow whispered. "You're home."

Home? Davy wondered silently to himself.

"This is your home now," Willow continued. "If you want it to be, that is. I've lived a full life here. Long enough to raise two kids and bury a husband. Just yesterday, I told Berma the Bench that I needed a new buddy. A roommate, rather. I have plenty of neighbors, but it's not the same in this big empty house. I'm calling you Davy because my husband's name was David. The second I saw you scampering up the hill, it gave me chills. David had beautiful black hair and green eyes, just like you. It's meant to be."

Davy looked around the room for a second time. Davy gathered by their glances that the jars of sand had been thinking the exact same thing. But if Davy had been sent to the white house for a reason, he didn't know what it was . . . yet.

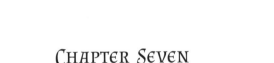

CHAPTER SEVEN

BERMA THE BENCH

Berma the Bench had been around for a long time. The creek animals called her the "Eyes of Trinity Trails" because she had seen and heard it all as the bench that once belonged to Mr. Whistler.

Berma sat beside her oldest and best friend, Oscar the Oak. They'd been together since the pre-park days and watched as Willow and David began construction on their home. Willow and David had been among the first to purchase land along the creek. Berma became a steady fixture in Willow's life, just as she had been in Mr. Whistler's. Berma celebrated milestones on good days and offered support on bad ones. She listened with a loving ear, extending compassion to every hard conversation.

Berma had loved watching Whistler Park grow. People couldn't wait to take their dogs out on the trails. The animals pranced as they passed one another. It had been Berma that coined the park walks "off the rails" in a nod to Mr. Whistler's vision of converting the railroad tracks to trail paths. Berma's sense of humor planted the seed for what would later become known as the weekly "Soul Train."

Every Wednesday at 7:00 a.m., during the prime-time morning stroll, the dogs competed in the "Water Cooler Walk-Off." They lined up in two rows, drank a sip of water, and, one by one, strutted down a line formed between the two rows. Berma and Oscar had a ringside seat from just up the trail. The birds fought for position and awarded a weekly winner. The winning dog had bragging rights all week.

Berma smiled as Willow and Davy approached.

"Morning, B," Davy said as he jumped onto his friend's back.

"Morning, D," Berma replied.

"Did I miss it?" Davy asked.

"Nope, you're right on time," Berma confirmed. Just then, Harley the Hummingbird zoomed by. Harley, on the other hand, was always late. Harley flew fast and furious to fight her way into the front row. Harley insisted on announcing the winning dog every week.

"I'm pulling for the Lab," Davy declared.

"Such a great idea," Berma bantered. "Totally worthy vote. While you're at it, let me know when the turtle crosses the creek."

"The Lab's got moves," Davy insisted. "If he wasn't so distracted he'd win every week. His ears perk up, and then he's *gone*. Maybe this time will be different."

"The Lab has NO shot," Berma emphasized. "The poodle will take it. She's best in show. The bangs play."

Berma, Oscar, and Davy watched the dogs line up. The Lab started strong but quickly lost focus, as predicted. The poodle pulled out a backward cowgirl dance move. She turned and scooted backward while bopping her arms like she was riding a horse. It was hilarious, but it, too, fell short. The winner of the week was the normally serious German Shepherd.

In a shocking stunt, and while standing on his hind legs, the Shepherd's front paws went from side to side, in front and then behind, popping in a zigzag motion. He popped all the way up to the line. He never smiled. He never broke from character. The Shepherd thrust his forelegs from side to side for three full seconds. He then fell back on all four feet and kicked his right hind leg to lock the performance. Harley called a clear victory, no contest.

"Definitely didn't see that coming," Davy declared, laughing.

"The Shepherd brought the house down," Berma agreed.

"Don't you wish you could shake that Lab?" Davy asked.

"Maybe it's stage fright," Oscar offered.

"Can't say," Berma abridged. "We're not here to judge."

Chapter Eight

The Barn Burner

Grey was ready for a nap. It had been an emotional morning, and she wanted to shake it off. Anne and Stan both left for work. Grey was enjoying the sudden quiet of the house. She was just beginning to doze off when she felt Lane's massive paw poke her.

"Don't even think about it," Lane said with a laugh.

"It's time to show you what this building is really made of. You need a tour of the amenities."

Grey had no idea what Lane meant. Nonetheless, she stood up and followed her roommate through the living room. Grey was shocked to see Lane open the front door. He motioned for her to walk into the hallway.

"After you," Lane said, smiling. Grey noted that Lane had offered no further explanation.

Grey was getting excited. She had started to worry that the city just consisted of distant strays and a snobby Bengal. Grey continued to follow Lane down the hallway and past the elevator. Nothing could have prepared Grey for where they went next.

Grey and Lane reached the neighbor's front door and were greeted by a poodle wearing a purple sequined poncho with the word *GOAT* written on the back. Purple fringe draped from the poodle's sides. Even her nail polish matched her poncho.

And the winner is, Grey thought to herself.

"TOPP!" Lane paw-bumped the grinning poodle. "Grey, meet Olivia. Olivia's the only other pet on our floor. I call her TOPP because she's the other penthouse's poodle. Olivia's the life and host of every party. She also happens to be the nicest dog you'll ever meet. She'll give you the poncho right off her back."

Grey saw Lane wink at Olivia. Grey wondered if Lane flirted with all of the dogs in the building. Grey laughed at the very thought of it.

"So nice to meet you, Grey!" Olivia offered. "You're going to love the Argos! You're just in time for this month's burner, which is perfect. Today it's just a casual get-together. There aren't any performances planned. Come on in—and let me know if you need anything."

Grey was trying very hard not to stare. Trying . . . and failing. Definitely failing. Olivia had a bowl haircut with blunt bangs and purple streaks that matched her toenail polish and poncho.

Some sections of Olivia's fur had been shaved, while other parts were kept long. The super long section swept the floor as she walked. Olivia's bright pink blush accentuated her naturally angular cheekbones. At a minimum, Grey could appreciate Olivia's total commitment to her look.

Grey entered the house and quickly realized Olivia was just the opening act for the residents that had gathered.

"That's Mikey," Lane whispered as they approached the next new face. At first glance, Mikey was a huge, white, long-haired cat wearing black plastic sunglasses and a bright green scarf. Mikey had wrapped the scarf around his neck and tied it to the side.

"What's up, Stripes?" Mikey asked in greeting. "You came with Anne, right?"

"Straight from the barn," Grey replied, grinning.

"Not much has changed then." Mikey laughed as he scanned the room. "You'll blend right in." Mikey tipped his glasses in Grey's direction and continued rotating around the room.

"Mikey's brilliant," Lane offered. "He's got one of those creative brains that just clicks on things the rest of us overlook. Mikey found those sunglasses in the dumpster. He never leaves the house without them."

"What's a burner?" Grey asked. "Olivia said this was a burner. She also mentioned performances."

"Olivia is a living performance," Lane said with a smile. "To answer your question, we have a monthly party so everyone can get together and catch up. Olivia calls it a burner. At some point, she'll ask if it's getting hot in here. That's her goal. She's known to turn up the volume. Olivia wants everyone to dress how they feel and dance to their own beat.

"Every other month, we open it up for residents to perform. You'd be surprised how much talent we have at the Argos. Olivia always hosts the party because she's got the perfect space. Plus, she's a social butterfly."

Grey took a moment to glance around the house. Each room had been painted a different color, with furniture to match. There was a blue dining room with blue plates and blue-and-black plaid chairs. A crystal light fixture hung above the dining table, casting rainbow sparkles all over the room. Next, Grey discovered a red piano room with pink-and-red-striped sofas. The piano was playing for a group of dogs that had gathered around it. The piano room led to an orange living room. The living room had large, orange glass butterflies dangling from the ceiling.

There was nothing traditional about this house, but Grey saw the genius. The house was designed to remind guests that they didn't need to conform. Every room was unique. It was almost as if the rooms themselves were telling Grey to go with the flow. All she had to do was find a spot that felt right for her.

Grey saw Blaze in the back of the living room. She walked over to say hello. Blaze was sitting with a miniature dog covered in tiny, delicate bows. Of course, the tiny dog was wearing a pearl collar.

"Grey, meet Meg." Blaze motioned to her bow-covered friend. "Meg is an award-winning Maltese breed, among many other things."

"Great to meet you, Meg," Grey replied.

"Likewise," Meg acknowledged. "Is it true that you lived in a barn? Bless your heart, this must feel so different for you. I hope you don't feel out of place here."

"Some things are definitely different," Grey acknowledged. "We generally avoid burning much in the country. Anytime a blaze gets out of hand, barn cats know how to put it out pretty fast."

Grey turned and walked back toward the front of the room. She knew she'd made her point. Grey saw Olivia laughing with Mikey. Mikey smiled in Grey's direction. Grey was beginning to see Mikey's point. Perhaps all buildings were barns. Some just looked fancier on the outside.

CHAPTER NINE
NO GUTS, NO GLORY

L ane had been watching Grey from the corner of
the room. Lane glanced at George the German
Shepherd and grinned. George was Lane's most
trusted confidante and a quick judge of character.

"Well, I guess that settles that," Lane roared. "Grey's
got guts. She may survive this city after all."

"No question she's got guts," George agreed. "No
guts, no glory. Just keep an eye on her. She'll be a threat

to some and a prize to others. In the beginning, it's going to be hard to *hear the difference.*"

Lane understood that George had made a point of emphasizing the last three words.

10

CHAPTER TEN

THE STAIRWELL

Blaze knew she was a trailblazer from the day she was born. That was how she got her name. Blaze opened her eyes as a kitten and announced on the spot that she had arrived. Watch out world, she had something to say. Contrary to public opinion, she preferred to say nice things. If Blaze couldn't think of something nice to say, she tried to say nothing at all.

Blaze had a look, and she played to it. She was covered in leopard-like caramel-colored spots. Blaze only weighed eleven pounds, but she was the beast of the building. The other animals at the Argos joked that they could see Blaze's shadow enter the room five minutes before she arrived. Her rhinestone collar wasn't subtle either. It bedazzled her whole body.

Blaze had her moments . . . her breaking points. The split-second reactions when her vulnerability sounded a lot like venom. When Blaze lost her temper, she also lost her cool. Deep down, she didn't mean any of it. Blaze was far more emotional than she could let on.

Blaze had lived with Stan for two years, but her broken heart would always belong to his mother, Jules. Blaze had loved her life with Jules. Jules treated Blaze more like a person than a pet. They watched TV, took naps, and played dress-up, all day, every day. Jules never left the house without loading up on every piece of jewelry she owned.

Blaze had been devastated when Jules handed her off to Stan. She would never understand. Jules *chose* not to take Blaze with her when she moved. Blaze learned to love Stan. She knew that Stan was a good person. Blaze worried that *she* wasn't a good enough pet. The whole situation had grown hazy in her head.

Blaze never talked about it, but she saw the brown box of her stuff every night when she closed her eyes to go to sleep. Her whole life had been reduced to that box. She had tried really hard to sweep the memory under the rug, where all pasts reside. She found it fitting that the rug was now off-limits.

Blaze knew one thing. She was never going to let it happen again. If Stan was in the room, she was there too. If Stan curled up on a blanket, she was in a ball beside him. Blaze knew that Stan needed the attention as much as she needed the assurance.

It was easier before Grey showed up. Blaze had a name for the years before Anne and Grey arrived. She called it her BAG phase: "Before Anne and Grey." Blaze had taken one look at Grey, and her heart hurt. She didn't care if Grey was the greatest roommate of all time. Blaze was terrified of being passed off once more. This was *her* home now.

Even still, Blaze had been embarrassed by Meg at the mixer. Meg had twisted Blaze's words. Blaze hadn't put Grey down or talked about her behind her back. She would never do that. It sure looked that way, though. Blaze wanted to explain, but everyone was watching. It wasn't the time or the place. Plus, Blaze wouldn't have blamed Grey for not believing her. Grey hadn't learned that sometimes one's reputation doesn't reflect their reality, especially in the city.

These were the thoughts that kept Blaze up every night. She'd always been a light sleeper, but it had gotten worse. Each night, she sat there until everyone else was asleep. Blaze waited until she could hear Stan and Lane snoring. Both of them, like bears. That was when she knew it was safe to sneak out of the bedroom. And the house.

Blaze had been a night roamer her whole life. Since she couldn't sleep, she used the time to think. Oftentimes, she'd overthink, but at least she was free to be. No one was watching her. She didn't have to be on her best behavior. Blaze could dance through the hallway and run down the stairs. She did both. The twilight hours were usually the highlight of her day. Unfortunately, that wasn't the case today. She couldn't shake the feeling in the pit of her stomach. It had been there since the party.

Blaze raced up and down the hallway for an hour before she decided to take the stairs. It was one of *those* nights—when night became morning. Blaze knew she could make it to the bottom of the stairs and back before anyone in her house stopped snoring. She had mastered this move. She ran to the door, jumped up, landed on the handle, and leaned forward. She had two seconds to slip through the slit before the door closed behind her. The stairwell watched Blaze blow by, all the way down, floor by floor.

The stairwell saw everything.

CHAPTER ELEVEN

SEVEN-LETTER WORD

D avy found comfort in being Willow's companion. He knew that Willow woke every morning with old memories on her mind. That's why it was her favorite time of day. The ghosts of her glory days visited her dreams, and by sunrise, she was ready to share her treasured gems.

Every day, Davy and Willow repeated the same pattern. First, they walked down the grassy hill to have a cup of coffee with Berma. Together, they watched squirrels race along the water's edge. The squirrels paused only to skip rocks and chase ducks. The red birds beckoned the butterflies to join, while Oscar blew a gentle breeze that carried the sweet scent of star jasmine from the garden.

Following coffee, they moved inside to sit on the ruffled sofa in the sunroom. The small room had become Davy's favorite spot in the house. It was cramped, with a glass table covered in outdated magazines, but perfectly positioned between the kitchen and the creek. The space smelled of pound cake, Willow's midmorning staple. It was here that Willow played crossword puzzles and told stories. Davy loved to listen. He nestled beside her on worn-out cushions as the sun trickled in through the windows.

"We met when I was twenty-one years old," Willow began.

Davy smiled. Willow always started with the same story.

"I had my whole life ahead of me," Willow continued. "David was five years older. I'll never forget the first time I saw him. He was standing in a hallway with his head cocked to the side. He just stood there and smiled at me. I knew right then that he was the sun and the moon for me. He lit up every direction I looked.

"David's hair hung over his forehead. It hid the scars and marks of mischief from a misspent youth, but nothing could hide the twinkle in his eyes. He was tall, thin, and muscular. Most of all, he was determined to do things at his own pace and on his own terms.

"I knew the universe put us together in that hallway for a reason. So, I waited. I waited for the life I knew we were supposed to share.

"It took time. All important things do. We eventually married and started a family. We built this big white house. We played games and laughed a lot. Thirty years went by in a blink.

"One day, his memory disappeared. I know the exact moment it happened. We were sitting right here on the sofa solving crossword puzzles. I realized we'd had the same conversation three times. He didn't remember it. His health faded shortly after his memory.

"I believe in my heart that David's waiting somewhere for us to solve crossword puzzles again. But you know what? I had to wait for him . . . and now it's his turn."

Davy saw Willow smirk at the very idea of her husband having to wait for her. Her eyes danced at her defiance. Then, like clockwork, Davy watched Willow's focus return to the puzzle in her hand.

"Davy, what's a seven-letter word for 'the road ahead'?" Willow winked as she looked to her sweet black cat for the answer.

Davy had heard the story of how Willow and David first met many times. Davy knew that Willow was lonely, and he needed advice on how to help her. Davy didn't know if he should sit quietly or push Willow to experience new things. Davy asked Berma for help.

Davy would never forget Berma's advice, or where her words of wisdom had come from. Berma read the sentence that Mr. Whistler had engraved on the brass badge on her back: "Honor the past but live in the moment. When it's time to move forward, pave a one-way street."

· · · · · · · ·

Davy wasn't accustomed to having people around him, but he was proud of Willow for stepping out of her comfort zone. Following the crossword puzzle, Willow had invited friends over. It was a tradition that David had started many years ago. David had always loved to entertain, and he never gave Willow any time to plan for it, either. David would wake up, and if the weather was nice, decide on a random group of friends to invite over. They'd watch the sun set over the creek and swap stories. David liked to introduce people who wouldn't normally meet. He called it his "Trail Mix"—a special blend of personalities that wouldn't have crossed paths without that one special night.

Davy remained in his bedroom for most of the party. He preferred the peace and quiet. Willow made a point of bringing a couple of her close friends to meet him. Davy's favorite person had been Jojo, the neighbor. Like Willow, Jojo and her husband had been among the first to purchase property on the trails. Jojo was a retired architect with a green thumb. She loved to plant in her garden.

"If there's one thing you can count on tonight, it's Jojo's overalls," Willow had warned. "Jojo keeps it real no matter who's around."

Willow was smiling from ear to ear when she brought Jojo into the room. Jojo had worn her denim overalls with a red-checkered tank top. Her cherry-red lipstick matched her shirt, and her white ringlet curls bounced as she walked. Davy noticed that even her work boots had flowers painted on them.

"Look at YOU!" Jojo exclaimed. "Well, you certainly do have David's style."

"I know, right?" Willow laughed. "David just would have been jealous that the cat's hair was thicker than his."

"Does David still appear?" Jojo softly inquired.

"Morning and night," Willow confirmed. "I see him in my dreams. Then I feel his presence around me in the mornings. I'm sure the kids would say that I'm drowning in the memories and grasping for ghosts, but it feels so real."

"What do you see?" Jojo asked. "What's David actually doing?"

"Waiting," Willow replied. "It feels like he's waiting for me to join him in *that* hallway. The one where we first met. The dream is always the same. Every night, I keep trying to reach it. I get close, and then I wake up."

"Maybe he's waiting for the day when you're both cats," Jojo said, smiling in Davy's direction.

Davy recognized that Jojo was trying to lighten the mood. Still, Davy felt as if he'd just gone from being the little black cat to the very large elephant in the room. Davy thought back on his day . . . from

Willow's dream to the crossword puzzle to the bigger issues of life and loss.

F-O-R-W-A-R-D, Davy thought to himself. *A seven-letter word for the road ahead is* forward.

Live in the moment.

12

THE TALKING STONE

Each day, Grey grew closer to finding her rhythm. Blaze had not spoken to Grey since the mixer, and she was happy to coexist in the quiet. Grey had heard from Lane that Blaze would be spending the afternoon at an Argos board meeting. The Argos board was a group of appointed animals that made decisions for all the pets in the building. With Blaze occupied by the meeting, Grey had the flexibility to explore every floor without the risk of running into Blaze or any of her friends.

Grey was on a mission to learn as much as she could about the Argos. She'd already discovered that the building was named after a dog, Argos, from ancient times. As the story was told, the dog had been owned by a warrior who went off to battle. He was gone for years and years, but the dog never lost faith that his owner would return. The dog sat and waited. The statue represented Argos's dedication and loyalty. Grey took pride in the fact that her building stood for something so special.

Grey knew there were only two homes on her floor. She also knew she was very lucky to live there. Their house belonged to Stan. Both Anne and Stan were a bit of a mystery to the other residents. They kept mostly to themselves.

Grey also learned that between the hours of 10:00 a.m. and 5:00 p.m., the animals had free rein over the Argos when their owners were at work. The other pets used this time to visit friends, but Grey took it upon herself to look behind each door and push every button in the building. She wanted to know who was hiding behind every curtain.

Each floor had a different energy. Grey noticed that on her floor, the homes lacked a ledge by their front doors. The hallways were quite boring. However, if she went one floor down, it was a totally different vibe, and it smelled like a secret garden. Every front door had a shelf with a flower arrangement. There must have been fifteen doors with fifteen vases. The hallway could have passed for a perfume bottle.

The artists lived on the seventh floor. It was by far Grey's favorite. The residents displayed trinkets and bowls filled with items they collected, which seemed to consist largely of crystal rocks. The crystals were mostly pink or purple. Grey had stopped to admire one bowl in particular when the front door opened. She tried to hide, but there was nowhere to go. She was caught between a rock and a hard place. In a brain and body mishap, her brain told her to sit, while her body told her to run. Grey somehow jumped from the doormat, to the wall, and back to the doormat again. She landed in the exact same spot. It wasn't until she landed that she noticed an old dog laughing in the doorway.

"Need some help?" the old dog inquired.

"I wasn't snooping," Grey apologized. "I'm new to the building. I'm trying to learn my way around. Each day, I visit a different floor to see how it's decorated. I was admiring your bowl. I didn't mean to pry. I promise. My name is Grey."

"Well, hello, Grey," the old dog said warmly. "My name is Crown. I'm a Cavalier King Charles Spaniel."

Grey saw that the dog had black fur on his ears and back. His underbelly was all white. He had tan-colored eyebrows, four black freckles, and a white spot on his forehead. The white spot actually looked like a crown of armor on the top of his head. Crown was wearing a black collar covered with turquoise beads, and his eyes were warm and welcoming.

"Which one caught your interest?" Crown pointed to his bowl on the ledge.

"The blue one," Grey replied. She pointed to a bright blue stone at the bottom of the bowl. The stone was buried underneath the others, and barely visible, which meant she *was* prying. Grey knew she'd just blown her own cover. She smiled smugly.

"What does the blue one stand for?" Grey asked. "I'm guessing each color has a meaning, right?"

"Good guess," Crown confirmed. "The blue stone represents your voice. When you keep it close, it's supposed to help you communicate what you're feeling. Would you like to have it?"

Grey felt her jaw drop. She noticed that Crown was smiling. Grey had a strange gut feeling, as though

Crown had been waiting for her to arrive. She knew that was impossible, but it seemed as though her visit had not come as a surprise at all. Grey couldn't figure out why she felt as if Crown knew more than he was letting on, or how she'd known to go straight for that blue stone.

"How long has the stone been sitting there?" Grey asked.

"It arrived yesterday," Crown replied. "My owner discovered it and brought it home. He said he knew the right person would come along and find it here. We added new rocks to the bowl last night."

Grey sat quietly for several minutes. She studied the dog in the doorway and decided to trust him.

"I don't need help with my voice," Grey finally replied. "It has power of its own. I can tell you about it, if you like."

Grey grinned as Crown invited her to come inside and share more. Grey had a hunch that Crown held the master key to many secrets in the building.

CHAPTER THIRTEEN
THE MINUTES

George stood before his fellow board members: Mikey the Long Hair, Meg the Maltese, Olivia the Poodle, and Blaze the Bengal. They had all gathered in the maintenance closet on the twenty-first floor. As chairman of the board, George called roll and raised his paw to lead their pledge.

I Pledge Allegiance,
To the Pets of the Argos Order of Loyalty,
And the Owners to Which We Commit,
Love, Licks, and Appreciation for All.

"I'd like to call the meeting of the Human Ownership Association, otherwise known as the 'HOA,' to order. We all know Crown is the official Argos Secretary. Crown's taking a few months off to rest, so I will continue to take notes in his absence.

"The first order of business today will be our next party," George began, reading the first item on the group's to-do list. "Olivia continues to extend her kind offer to host the building mixers in her home. As we all know, this is extremely generous. She handles the setup and cleanup. Our next mixer will include an open mic invitation for Argos performances. We should expect a full house. We always have a large crowd when we build a stage. For that reason, I'd like to suggest we have a bouncer at Olivia's door. Do we have any nominations?"

"I nominate Moosey the Bernese Mountain Dog on the fourth floor," Mikey volunteered. "Moosey's been pushing me to let him participate. If you haven't seen him lately, he's enormous. Moosey can guard the door and prevent any potential problems. He'll do whatever Olivia wants."

"I second that nomination," Olivia noted for the record.

"Terrific!" George exclaimed. "Thank you both! I'll reach out to Moosey this week.

"Next up, let's discuss our dwindling number of animals. We all know we've had a few super-great humans move out this year. We want to keep our reputation as the best and most animal-friendly building in the city. Does anyone have any ideas on how to reach new residents? I know we all have friends in other buildings. We'd love to see them make a move over to the Argos, right?"

"I nominate Meg and myself to handle this," Blaze offered. "We know the kind of animals that we'd all like to see move in. We can create flyers and drop them on the Trinity Trails to advertise to potential residents. If animals live nearby, they'll be on the trails. The simplest approach is to promote the building to people that already know the area. The animals can then steer their owners in the right direction."

"I second that nomination," Meg confirmed.

"Great!" George noted. "The final item for discussion is building security. We all know we're lucky to live here, but we can't take our situation for granted.

More and more, there are animals without homes. We must take extra precaution to protect ourselves. I'll give this more thought in the coming weeks, and for our next meeting, I'll come prepared to suggest new safety measures. I'd love to hear your ideas too. That's all I have for today. Does anyone want to make a motion to end the meeting?"

"Absolutely!" Blaze belted out. "I make a motion to adjourn the meeting."

George grinned.

"I second that motion," Mikey offered.

"All in favor, say 'I,'" George requested.

"I!" the group shouted in unison.

George made a note that all attendees of the board meeting had agreed to call it a day. He watched each animal leave the room. It wasn't the only note that George wrote down.

. . . .

George had a thick coat of black-and-tan fur, strong bones, and deep brown eyes that watched every single thing around him. He knew he was a purebred German

Shepherd and the primary animal in charge at the Argos. He just didn't think of himself that way. George thought of himself as a regular dog. This crossed his mind in every board meeting, as he caught himself wondering how in the world he reached the head of the table, so to speak. His first memories of life flashed through his mind each time he read the pledge aloud.

George was born into a litter of four to a family that couldn't afford to keep them. The other three puppies had been personable and playful. George wasn't. He was a thinker. He didn't jump on command. He didn't roll over on cue. Instead, he studied his siblings' reactions and decided whether he would have done the same thing. George was highly intelligent, and he analyzed everything.

George always played by a different set of rules. It was for these reasons that he wasn't the first pick of his litter. Or the second, or the third. In fact, George wasn't picked at all. Humans couldn't figure him out. He scared them off. They all agreed that George was the strongest and smartest of the four puppies, but they worried that George was too independent to become a family dog. As a result, he was taken to a nearby shelter.

George learned a lot in those early days at the shelter. He learned to listen and watch. George saw the other dogs bark over one another when potential owners visited. The dogs yelped for anyone. George didn't think less of the other dogs for their barking. He just wished more for them. He wanted all of the animals at the shelter to find the home that was really meant for them.

George waited for the right person to come along. Quietly and patiently, George waited. He never barked. Not once. Even when the days turned to months.

George was sleeping when Mr. Hughes finally arrived at the shelter. George would later learn that Mr. Hughes was a retired detective who had spent most of his life solving cases and analyzing clues. It was a perfect match. Mr. Hughes had a big, wide smile and honey-colored hair. He was looking for a smart and trainable dog that could keep his mind active in retirement.

George's shelter was the first and only one that Mr. Hughes visited. Apparently, Mr. Hughes had walked straight over to George's cage and sat down. George would never forget the minute he opened his eyes. He had immediately barked—for himself, for Mr. Hughes, for joy.

George gathered his notes and collected his thoughts. In honor of his humble beginnings, George barked as he left the room en route to visit Olivia.

. . . .

George couldn't help but smile at Olivia. They came from entirely different worlds, and most days, it felt as if they spoke totally different languages. While George was serious, Olivia was sassy. They were both headstrong, but George greatly admired Olivia's work ethic and her ongoing commitment to the Argos residents.

George knew that Olivia would leave the board meeting and promptly begin planning the details for the upcoming mixer. So he wasn't surprised when she informed him that she'd already decided that it *must* be a costume party.

"Look, George, I know parties," Olivia said. "You're in charge of security. I'm in charge of the vibe. I know what's at stake, but I still need to set the tone. We've had a hard time getting the residents to let loose. The whole point of planning for these get-togethers is to deepen our relationships. If everyone's putting up a front, it's a dud before we open the door. Costumes help animals chill out. Plus, I'm bringing in the big guns to set up a stage. It will be amazing. You're going to have to trust me."

"OK, OK," George relented and waved goodbye with a grin. "It's your house, your party, and your plan. I'm off to walk the building."

George didn't know much about housewarming or hosting. However, he knew every square inch of the building. He walked it every day. He'd learned a lot from Mr. Hughes. He knew how to find patterns. George also knew not to overlook the obvious. The smallest detail could change everything.

George began at the bottom of the building and took the stairs all the way up. He stopped on each floor to make sure the security cameras and light bulbs were working. He looked for anything suspicious. He'd noticed a few weeks prior that two light bulbs were out on the first floor. Without those lights, the back door to the building was pitch dark at night.

Getting the light bulbs changed was a priority item on his to-do list.

George had always been observant. Mr. Hughes simply sharpened his skills. George spent just two months in training. Even Mr. Hughes had been surprised by how quickly George learned cues and commands. However, George's basic instincts hadn't come from training. He had always had a unique ability to see things on the horizon.

George generally had a minute-by-minute plan before anyone else knew they even needed one, or where to look.

CHAPTER FOURTEEN

SIGNS

Polly watched Merak move into position. Merak was hiding behind a blinking streetlight. Polly knew that Merak, in particular, loved dropping in on the action to animal watch. Normally, Polly gave Merak this "me" time for herself. Today was not a normal day.

Polly knew that within minutes, two dogs would cross paths. Polly knew it because the stars arranged for it to happen. The two dogs, strangers to each other, had no clue that this single moment in their day would change the course for so many other animals. Polly saw Merak tickle the streetlight, causing the yellow light to squirm. The red light laughed and lit up.

A blond runner with a matching blond Goldendoodle stopped abruptly at the now red light. The Goldendoodle's nose turned toward the large green shrubs lining the sidewalk. Polly and Merak saw the exact moment the Goldendoodle made eye contact with the mystery dog.

"Let the show begin," Merak whispered.

Polly laughed as the blond Goldendoodle twisted her neck so the streetlight would bounce off the gold studs on her collar. Then, with her right paw, the Goldendoodle brushed back the curls in her fur while she fluttered her long lashes. Polly appreciated the dog's ability to be flirty and fabulous, all within fifteen seconds.

Polly saw the light change from red to green. The runner and her striking Goldendoodle raced to the tall building just down the road. Polly smirked as the dog in the shrubs followed behind. The dog carefully maneuvered between the plants to remain hidden. Polly watched the dog pause when he reached the cross street at the back of the Goldendoodle's building. The dog seemed to be staring at the "Eagle Landing" street sign.

Polly squinted to see the dog dart from the shrubs. The dog caught the door just before it closed behind the sassy Goldendoodle. Polly watched Merak dance with delight.

"Might as well be a bull's-eye," Polly deadpanned.

15

CHAPTER FIFTEEN
WEEKLY SESSION

L ane gently tapped the door at unit 713. He was right on time for his weekly visit. Lane smiled as his old friend invited him inside.

"How're you doing?" Lane asked. Lane was aware that some days were better than others. Recovering from surgery was never easy, especially at Crown's age.

"What do I always tell you?" Crown countered. "You wake up each day with a choice. Choose to be happy.

The bandages are off. I probably won't walk the trails again, but I've been given the gift of time. I spend my afternoons with friends. I'm working on special projects. What more could I possibly need?"

Lane helped Crown scoot to his favorite spot by the window. They sat down together, side by side. The room was filled with special items—items that Crown's owner collected. Lane looked around at the latest assortment of feathers and stones. He noticed a new wind chime had been hung on the patio.

Crown and his human were "healers"—which meant they helped other people heal from stress. Lane didn't quite understand how it all worked, but he liked talking to his friend each week. Lane always left Crown's house feeling lighter and more like himself. Lane and Crown usually spent the visit talking about anything new that had occured in Lane's life. Lane was hoping to take the conversation in a new direction today.

"What did you think of Grey?" Lane began. "She told me she met a new friend. She showed me the blue stone. It was nice of you to give her that. She carries it everywhere. It meant a lot to her."

"Grey's a rock star," Crown chuckled.

"Oh, you're on today!" Lane laughed.

"She's got an interesting tale," Crown continued. "It took a lot of work for her to arrive at the Argos. Grey told me that she knew in her heart she was destined to be here. She's excited to meet friends. I'll be honest, it's refreshing to see the building through her eyes. Grey has no hidden agenda. What you see is what you get."

"Why did you choose the blue rock for her?" Lane inquired. "I've never seen it before."

"I didn't choose it," Crown clarified. "I sensed someone standing outside the apartment, so I opened the door. Grey was hovering in the hallway. She's been walking every floor to get more familiar with the layout of the building. Grey paused to look at the bowl on our ledge. I asked her if something specific had caught her attention. She pointed to the blue rock. It was meant to be. In that moment, the stone belonged to her. So, I suggested that she take it."

"Why do you think Grey wanted that one, though?" Lane wondered. "Favorite color? Did it remind her of someone from the farm? Did she say anything?"

Lane sensed that Crown knew more than he was telling.

"What about you?" Crown redirected the conversation. "How are *you* doing this week? How are your ears?"

"I'm fine," Lane replied with a laugh. "My ears are fine. Everything's fine. At least, it would be if I could tune out the constant background noise from the trails."

"Maybe there's a reason you hear it?" Crown inquired.

"The strays steal to survive," Lane barked.

"How could they not?" Crown urged. "What would *you* do to survive?"

"They can't be trusted," Lane insisted. "Besides, we were both taught to ignore them. This isn't just me. It's been the policy among the leashes since way before I arrived. Just because I can hear inner thoughts doesn't mean I can be responsible for everyone's problems. I made a commitment when I arrived at the Argos to focus my gift on helping fellow leashes. Does that make me a hero or a villain? And how do you choose the one exception to the rule when there are so many shouting for attention?"

"By listening," Crown coached.

"Have *you* been listening?" Lane countered. "I hear everything."

"You hear those you can help," Crown clarified.

"Let's talk about helping Grey," Lane insisted. "Blaze hasn't exactly rolled out the red carpet. I can't hear any of Grey's thoughts, which makes me think she doesn't need me. However, I still want to know that she's settling in OK. Did Grey share anything with you?"

"Grey chose a blue stone," Crown acknowledged. "Blue stones represent voice. Perhaps you start there.

Try listening instead of hearing. I've been telling you for years that they aren't the same thing. Fear speaks up, power projects, but needs often remain silent until it's too late. Right now, Grey needs a family. She seeks familiarity. That's probably the only thing Grey can't make happen on her own. It's also the one item she can't bear to think about. That's likely why you can't hear anything from her."

Lane noticed a gentle concern in the creases of Crown's face.

"Grey sees the strays as symbolic of her past," Crown concluded. "She's got to learn to see the leashes as her family now, and that's a big leap for a former barn cat. It isn't easy to leave your past for your present, even when your present is everything you dreamt about."

"Sounds like I've got a roommate that needs attention," Lane said, relenting.

"Don't forget about Blaze," Crown cautioned.

"I hear you," Lane countered as he rolled his eyes.

*Try listening
instead of
hearing.*

16

CHAPTER SIXTEEN
THE BRONZE BROCHURE

Blaze was growing impatient with Meg. Blaze had given Meg a very simple task: decorate the page; make it look interesting. Blaze couldn't figure out why her friend was making it so hard.

"Look, we're going to strategically plant these fly-ers on the Trinity Trails," Blaze explained . . . *again*. "I'm going to drop a brochure with the flick of a wrist as I pass by in the stroller. If I roll it tight enough, it will squeeze right through the mesh lining. They don't have to be perfect. They just have to capture the right animals' attention. We know what they need to say. Start by drawing a picture of the bronze Argos statue at the building entrance.

"Argos represents loyalty and commitment. The dog waited years to be reunited with his owner. He is literally lying at his human's feet. The statue shows the kind of relationships and respect that we have for one another, and for our owners. It's the symbol of the building. No one overlooks it. We also have to make sure we include details about the building itself. You do understand who we're trying to reach, don't you?"

Hearing the sound of her own voice, Blaze immediately felt guilty by her tone.

"I understand the target audience," Meg affirmed, clearly offended. "I'm going to draw a picture of the trails, the Argos statue, and the board. We need to spotlight the animals behind the scenes. The board is responsible for bringing everyone together for parties and fun. It makes sense to feature them on the brochure."

"I agree," Blaze replied. "The brochure should showcase the whole package. What if you put the Argos symbol at the top of the page too? The logo with the A and the dog. And underneath it, write 'Where Loyalty Lives.'"

"That's good," Meg mused.

"Underneath the logo, list the top talking points about the building: walking distance to the Trinity Trails, mixers with the residents," Blaze continued.

"Done and done," Meg replied. "By the way, I think we're our best advertisement. How do we look?"

Blaze burst out laughing when Meg held up the brochures. Meg wasn't exactly an artist, but she'd gotten the job done. That's all that mattered. Blaze decided it was better that the brochure looked like a crafts project. It was more personal that way.

Blaze organized the brochures into a neat stack as Meg gossiped about next steps and who would wear what to the upcoming mixer. Blaze listened and laughed as she carefully added costume details and special notes to the top page.

"Careful, Meg," Blaze said, beaming. "Loose lips sink ships."

CHAPTER SEVENTEEN

TURN OF EVENTS

Grey watched Anne put her book down.

"Blaze," Anne called out. "Grey and I are on the sofa. Come sit with us."

Grey knew that Blaze wouldn't come. Still, every Thursday, Anne called for her and hoped for a different outcome. On Thursdays, Stan and Lane went to the ranch and returned late. Anne used those nights to curl up on the couch, read, and reflect on all the things she was thankful for. Grey always sat beside Anne, but sadly, Blaze refused to join.

"I keep thinking back to my first spring break at BMF," Anne admitted. "For some reason, it's been on my mind all day. All of my friends had gone to the beach, and I was forced to go to Black Mountain Farm. I fought with Uncle Joe for three solid days. And on the fourth, he taught me to ride the four-wheeler."

Grey smiled at the memory of Miss Mule. Grey had heard parts of this story before.

"That was the day that changed everything," Anne continued. "The day I met Miss Mule. We started on the trails closest to the main house and didn't stop until we'd gone from one side of the mountain to the other. That particular day was damp. The mud from the trails covered my skin like cake batter. The dewy honeysuckle sweetened the air like sugar. I'd tasted adventure, and I was hooked.

"I learned how to smile that week. My friends returned from the beach with a tan. I came back from the farm with a glow. I had a fresh new perspective on what it meant to feel free. Free to explore, free to get dirty, and free to have FUN. From then on, I was always disappointed by anyone that couldn't hold their own on a muddy road.

"I've always felt that same freedom with Stan. I didn't think twice when he asked me to move in. It was a no-brainer. So was redecorating."

Grey watched Anne pause from the story to take a sip of her drink. She saw Anne grin as she placed the cup back on a coaster.

"He told me to make myself at home," Anne clarified. "I told him to be careful what he wished for! I hung photos from the farm first. They're my reminders, my home away from home. Don't you just love Gabby the Goat? I always imagine that she's greeting me with coffee in the morning. It's a start. I have to be patient. It'll take time for this place to feel like it's mine too. Ours, actually."

Grey leaned in to acknowledge Anne's sentiment.

"I always go back to what Uncle Joe said that day I met Miss Mule. He told me that life's a marathon, not a sprint. You can't go too fast. You have to learn how to safely drive first. Some days will be muddy; other days will be sunny. You need to be able to switch gears and adjust to safely ride them both. It's called the road to compromise. Once you get the hang of it, there's no stopping you. You can turn the wheel and rest assured you're ready to go in either direction, wherever life takes you."

Grey rested against Anne and purred. Minutes felt like hours. Anne motioned that it was time for bed. Grey jumped from the sofa and headed for the hallway.

"Good night, Gabby," Grey whispered as she passed the happy goat.

. . . .

Grey had been standing on Anne's chest for fifteen minutes. Grey was fully rested after their girls' night. As it turned out, so was Anne . . . so much so that Grey couldn't shake her out of bed. The sound of Lane barking in the kitchen finally broke through.

Grey watched Anne dart to get dressed. Grey had a feeling that Stan and Lane had been late getting home. She saw that Lane was moving slowly. Blaze, on the other hand, seemed ahead of schedule. Grey noticed that Blaze was already sitting in the stroller by the front door.

"Know anything about that?" Lane asked. He nodded his head in Blaze's direction.

"Nope," Grey replied. "We didn't see Blaze last night. You know that if Stan isn't around, neither is Blaze."

Grey could see that Lane was concerned. Grey wondered what about this morning was causing him to pause and take notice. Grey was about to ask when Anne made a beeline for the front door. Grey crawled into the stroller, careful not to disturb Blaze. Grey noticed that Blaze didn't budge.

"Blink, Blaze," Grey requested. "I'll assume you're OK, if you just blink."

Blaze blinked but didn't say a word.

Grey noted that Blaze didn't move the entire trip out to the trails. In fact, Blaze repositioned herself only when they turned around at the water cooler. At that exact moment, Blaze dropped her shoulder and rolled over inside the stroller. Grey found it odd because she'd never seen Blaze roll over for anything before.

Grey also saw that a group of strays had gathered along the trail. The strays stood shoulder to shoulder, lined up in a row. Grey glanced at Lane and noticed that he was staring straight ahead.

Grey's heart hurt. Grey could feel her former family watching as she rode en route to her shiny, glass house. Grey knew she wasn't a stray, but she couldn't shake the fear that she had somehow become a traitor. Three weeks ago, Grey was a barn cat, no better than the faces lining the trails before her.

"Feed them," Grey whispered through the mesh lining on the left side of the stroller. Grey watched her words dart through the air, tipping the food dispensers from pole to pole. Nourishment and love showered the strays from every direction. It was the first time Grey had used her voice in the city. The magic fed her soul as much as it fed the strays.

Grey slowly turned to face Blaze, who seemed oblivious to Grey's grand gesture. Blaze appeared pre-occupied with the paper littering their path. Grey took a deep breath, thrilled that Blaze's high-brow snobbery had actually worked in her favor for a change.

· · · · · · · ·

Grey agreed to follow Lane into the study. She watched Lane close the door behind them. At first, Grey was scared that Lane had seen her big move on the trails. Instead, and to Grey's delight, Lane carefully placed a handful of items on Stan's cluttered desk.

"Take a seat," Lane suggested as he motioned to Stan's chair. "We have to prepare you for the upcoming mixer. If you can find a real instrument that's been donated to the dumpster, grab it fast. Those are hot commodities around here. Otherwise, the Argos animals play the pantry. You have to get creative. Percussion can be accomplished on bowls, cans, or jars. Personally, I prefer empty jam jars and soup cans. They produce a deeper ring sound.

"Recycled water bottles work when you want to create a horn. You cut a couple of holes along the bottle and cover them with your paws. When you blow into the bottle, move your paw to make different sounds. The horns require the most practice, but we have some very talented pets. If you don't want to put that much time and energy into it, then toss Anne's loose change in a jar. It'll sound like a tambourine when you shake it."

Lane demonstrated by dropping coins into the jar he'd been playing. He then placed a lid on top. Grey watched Lane shake around the room with the newly made tambourine.

Grey stared at the forks, jars, and glasses on the table. In her wildest imagination, she hadn't seen this coming.

"Does every animal play an instrument?" Grey asked, nervous she would fall short.

"Not at all," Lane answered. "We have a couple of singers here, too."

"That's my jam," Grey said, and smiled.

"Do you have a good voice?" Lane laughed.

"Some might call it magic." Grey grinned.

"I'm all ears," Lane said with a smirk. "That's if you're not afraid of singing a cappella. Can you belt out a solo without instruments backing you up?"

Grey glanced around the room, searching for inspiration to accept Lane's dare. She smiled at the photos of Stan on the ranch. They reminded her of Anne's hallway homage to the farm. She closed her eyes and thought of the sun beaming through the barn.

Every picture,
The frames,
Every ray of light,
Reflects on you.
And the memory,
Of where I
Used to be,
You follow me.

"Just a little ditty for the dog?" Lane winked. "You're a shark in cat's clothes! That was amazing! What else do I need to know? Do you have wings to go with that voice?"

"My words don't need wings to fly," Grey said as she sat back down beside Lane. "In fact, there's something I think you should know."

"What's up?" Lane inquired.

Grey paused, her throat suddenly tight with nerves.

"I fed the strays today," Grey whispered. Grey watched Lane's eyes harden.

"What do you mean, you fed the strays?" Lane replied. "How?"

"Singing aside, I really do have a magical voice. My words can do anything I tell them to. They'll take any shape and perform any action as long as I'm using them for good."

Grey paused. She expected a hero's welcome. She was shocked that Lane didn't seem impressed. Grey noticed that Lane was growing more serious by the minute.

"How?" Lane repeated.

"I directed my words to feed them. I watched the words fly through the air like a gust of wind. They knocked food from the dispensers."

"How is that for the greater good?" Lane demanded. "You fed ferals today!"

"I fed strays today!" Grey corrected him. "Hungry, homeless strays that could be my *family*! I can't ignore them. I won't!"

"*We* are your family!" Lane exclaimed. "You're a leash now, unless that's just a collar you wear when it's convenient."

Grey watched Lane pace the room. She found it odd that he kept pausing to swipe at his ears. Grey wondered if Lane was getting sick. She was worried about him.

"I know I'm a house cat," Grey said with a sigh. "I just don't want other animals to suffer."

"You don't think I know how hard it is to turn your back?" Lane barked. "Grey, I have a secret gift too. I have magical ears! Let that one soak in for a second. I hear the inner thoughts of animals in need. You can't even imagine what the trails sound like for me!"

"What do you hear?" Grey gasped. She'd asked the question, but she wasn't sure she could bear the answer. Grey noticed that Lane suddenly looked very sad.

"Please tell me," Grey urged.

"Every animal is different," Lane relented. "Sometimes I hear the whisper of hope. Those animals seek reassurance. Sometimes I hear fear. Those animals seek silence. Fear is almost always louder than hope. But we all make choices. You can't help everyone. There isn't enough of you to go around. I chose to champion the leashes. If you live in this building, it's a choice you'll have to make too. Granted, no one's path is the same . . . but mark my words, sooner or later, you're going to reach a fork in the road. I hope for your sake that you turn to the right side."

Grey grabbed a fork and tapped it against an empty jam jar. The sound rung like the bell after a boxing match. Grey wasn't sure who had won, but she was done with the conversation.

18

CHAPTER EIGHTEEN
THE PRACTICE ROUND

Olivia spent the morning thinking about the first Argos mixer she hosted. There had been no expectations . . . just a small group of friends, each of whom contributed something. Treats or toys, they kept it simple.

Olivia laughed to herself. This was bound to happen eventually. She was born to make things big. After all, she'd performed as a competitive poodle since she could walk. Any victory, big or small, had been won by attention to detail. The practice behind the performance led to the illusion of greatness.

Olivia had mastered it all, and she had the blue ribbons to show for it. But times had changed. She now dared any animal to compete with her event planning. Olivia's parties were known as "hot spots" of preparation. That's how the name "burner" had come to her in the first place.

Olivia brought honest energy to every event. She worked hard at reminding herself to be natural. Natural didn't mean that she couldn't wear purple nail polish. It meant that the purple nail polish was a natural choice for her. Olivia used the parties as a venue to encourage the Argos residents to let their true colors rock out too.

"I want the flowers to follow you into every room," Olivia directed the event crew that had gathered for rehearsals. "I want this to be completely over the top. Let's blow the roof off this one."

The crew laughed. They knew that when Olivia had an idea, there was no stopping her.

"This will be quite the setup," the head of the event team replied. "We can't have any delays."

"I agree," Olivia confirmed. "If you can pull it off, I think it makes sense for you to stay overnight. I would never normally suggest that, but this party is special."

"We'll find a way," the team replied.

Olivia signed the contract on what was sure to become her most talked about event. This burner would move animals beyond words. She walked from room to room, detailing every single step. Illusion was everything.

19

CHAPTER NINETEEN
WILD, WILD WEST

George knocked on the door and smiled. He didn't do costumes, but he had a hunch that his friends wouldn't disappoint. George was shocked to see Blaze open the door. He was even more surprised to see that she'd dressed up for the party . . . as a sheriff.

George was blown away by the level of detail in Blaze's costume. She had cut the foot out of one of Stan's old navy socks, stretched it out as wide as it would go, and was wearing it as a body armor police vest. She'd also taken a thin blue tie, wrapped it around her neck, and tucked the ends into the sock. Blaze had attached one of Stan's silver pins to the tie. The pin had a star engraved in the metal. Blaze even made a fake sheriff's badge and placed it in Stan's old wallet. She flipped it open to show George. George then noticed that Blaze was carrying silver handcuffs as a prop. George didn't ask how Blaze got them.

"There's a new sheriff in town," Blaze said with a smirk.

"I must have missed that update in the last board meeting," George replied. "Does this mean you'll be overseeing security in the building? Can I take a break?"

"You know I'm more concerned with the admissions process," Blaze bantered. "We can't keep letting just anyone in the building."

George caught Blaze's not-so-subtle point as she looked in Grey's direction to emphasize the word "admissions." George followed Blaze's voice into the living room, where he promptly and involuntarily laughed out loud. George lost it the second he saw Grey and Lane. The two were dressed as a country western duo: a cowgirl and her horse.

"Howdy, partner," Grey drawled.

George grinned. "Howdy, slick! You can take the girl out of the country, but you can't take the country out of the girl."

George watched Grey do a full spin to show off her costume. George noticed that Grey had cut a head and two armholes in one of the tan-colored cloth bags Anne used to store her shoes. It had given Grey just enough of an opening to pull the small bag over her head. Grey had clearly cut the garment to land at her knees. She'd then glued spaghetti noodles around the collar and hemline to look like matching fringe. The stiff noodles were all lined up in perfect rows that swished back and forth as Grey moved.

"This cowgirl found the goods," Grey declared, as she pointed to the turquoise necklaces stacked around her neck and the rope tied in a western knot around her waist. "A pop of color and a touch of rope—what more could I need?"

George realized that the remainder of the rope had been used as a harness prop for Lane.

"From Anne's closet to the maintenance closet, I presume," George said, laughing.

George saw that Lane had taken a simpler approach to his look. Lane had clearly joined Grey in raiding the maintenance closet, where it appeared that he'd painted an empty paper towel roll to match his chocolate-colored fur and secured it on his nose in a long horse shape. Lane had also painted a bath mat, draped it over his back, and written "Howdy" on the makeshift seat. George didn't bother to ask from whose bathroom Lane had stolen that mat.

"So, we've got a sheriff and a lone ranger, huh?" George asked the group. "I suppose we'll have to work out who the Argos outlaws are."

"You never really know, do you?" Grey smirked. "What have you got there?"

Grey pointed to the envelope George was carrying.

"Oh, I forgot I was even carrying it," George joked. "I tried to stop by Crown's house on the way here, but he didn't answer the door. These are his board meeting notes. Mind if I leave them here during the party? I'll swing back through afterward to pick them up."

"Sure thing," Lane said, nodding. "Drop it in Stan's office. He has stacks of paper; it'll fit right in."

"I was going to suggest the same thing," George said. He walked through the home quickly. George turned into the study and paused to look around. Stan's old ranch books lined the shelves from wall to wall. They carried the smell of cowboys' cologne, a distinct combination of aged paper and worn leather mixed with good old-fashioned sweat. George knew the study was the only room that had not been redecorated when Anne moved in. It felt like the last remaining saloon.

How apropos, George thought to himself.

George approached Stan's favorite lounge chair and ottoman. He saw a loose paper underneath the ottoman and leaned down to pick it up. The paper had a hand-drawn picture of the Argos dog statue. George noticed that the paper also named the Argos board members and referenced the Trinity Trails. It even mentioned the mixer and the day's date. George guessed that it was one of Blaze's brochures. He grabbed the brochure, flipped it over, and wrote as quickly as he could. He stuffed the sheet of paper in the envelope he was holding for Crown. George carefully placed the envelope underneath the ottoman. He could hear the group calling for him to hurry.

"Don't let me forget to grab that envelope for Crown after the party," George whispered to Grey. "I stuffed it under Stan's ottoman to be safe. Be sure to remind me."

Chapter Twenty
The Big Topp

Grey's entire body was shaking with excitement. She passed the blinking light of the elevator and rounded the corner to Olivia's front door. Then she stopped. They all did: Grey, George, Lane, and Blaze. They all came to a screeching halt.

Grey hadn't dared to try to anticipate Olivia's costume. There was no way to guess and no reason to try. But if the Argos animals had placed bets on the costume of choice for the bouncer at Olivia's door, no one, not a single one of them, would have bet on Moosey as a massive ballerina.

Grey knew that under Moosey's thick brown, black, and white coat, he was actually a gentle giant. A giant . . . with fierce dance moves that could pull off a pink tutu and pearls without missing a beat. Grey could tell that Moosey was equally proud of his costume and his role at the party.

Grey approached Moosey at the front door and saw that he was holding a binder. Grey read the words *Master RSVP List* on the binder's spine. Moosey appeared to be checking off every animal's name as they entered Olivia's home.

Grey and Lane were the first of their group to step inside. They each thanked Moosey as he crossed their names off the list. Grey wondered if she'd just landed on a different planet. Grey spotted the red and white roses first. At first glance, it looked like tall bursts of flowers had been placed in every room and on every table. The roses appeared to be working the rooms as a team.

The white roses seemed to act as the welcoming committee. Grey noticed that their job was to greet and guide animals throughout the house. Grey quickly concluded that the red roses were there to make sure no one stepped out of line. The flower arrangements had been placed in rows to create the illusion of red and white stripes. They were all lined up, white following white and red after red. Grey then realized this was just the start to Olivia's party theme: Circus Argos.

Grey paused to take it all in. Red and blue lights flashed from room to room, and each room seemed to spotlight a different act. Olivia had transformed the blue dining room into her very own fortune-teller extravaganza. Olivia was sitting in the center of the table with a crystal ball and a deck of cards. She was wearing a white dress with purple satin stripes along the sides and a matching purple scarf wrapped around her head. The chandelier reflected on candles that covered the table. Grey saw that Olivia was in the process of reading the future for Frank, a French Bulldog new to the building. Grey caught Olivia's eye and winked.

"Crown usually reads the cards," Lane whispered. "He's great at it. Olivia's just filling in for fun while he recovers. I wouldn't plan your life around how she reads those cards. Just saying."

Grey and Lane were both eager to see the main stage. Both of their jaws dropped the second they entered the living room. A circus tent had been erected with red and white sheets. The sheets were draped from one side of the room to the other, hanging from the exposed pipes on the high ceiling. The ceiling's track lighting had been redirected to shine on the stage in the middle of the room. The stage was also covered in red and white sheets. A brown wooden table had been placed in the middle of the stage.

Grey saw that Mikey was standing behind the table, tapping his paw and rocking his head back and forth to the beat.

"Mikey found a record player and a bunch of old records in the dumpster," Lane explained. "With practice, he taught himself how to spin the records. We made him the official Argos DJ for all parties. His stage name is Music Mike."

Grey saw that Mikey's records were stacked in two piles on each side of his record player. Grey assumed the next record in rotation was the one Mikey had already pulled out. She laughed as she read the words *Cat Scratch Fever* on its cover.

Mikey was wearing a blue denim Western shirt with pearl snap buttons. He'd left the top two buttons unsnapped. Mikey had also wrapped an orange bandana around his neck and tied the ends off to the side. Grey could tell that Mikey would be a very tough act to follow.

Grey and Lane walked to the food station next. Grey knew that everyone in the building had contributed to the buffet. Olivia spent the week prior to the event stopping by each attendee's house. As an entry fee, every animal was expected to provide a cup of their favorite treats. The treats were all combined and served on party platters. Earlier that week, Olivia had explained to Grey that she wanted each animal to feel included in the planning process. It also gave the guests something to talk about.

"These are Olivia's contribution," Lane warned as he pointed to the dry crackers. "They're all-natural. Olivia loves them, but they're an acquired taste. By that, I mean they have no taste. It's like licking the floor."

"Good to know," Grey said, laughing.

"This place is packed," Lane observed. "Everyone showed up today."

Grey surveyed the room and studied the other costumes. Grey saw that Meg had used red lipstick to write a big "S" on a hand towel. The towel looked like one of Anne's "show towels" that no one was supposed to touch. Meg had wrapped the small towel around her body and clasped it together with bows.

SuperDog, Grey thought, smiling to herself. She laughed as Meg strutted across the room to speak to a Greyhound. From Grey's daily adventures, she knew the Greyhound lived on the seventh floor and was rumored to be dating a Goldendoodle. The Greyhound had wrapped himself in foil and had written *Kiss* with a Sharpie. Grey pointed out the Greyhound to Lane. "That's a big bite of chocolate," Grey said, giggling.

They watched the lights flicker as Olivia stepped onto the stage. "Circus Argos is in the HOUSE!" Olivia screamed. "As many of you know, it is my great pleasure to host these mixers. We're so lucky to live here among friends. I'm honored to have such a huge crowd with us today. I hope you all have a chance to meet someone new. Don't forget to give a shout out to our very own resident DJ: Music Mike! Let's get this party started!"

The whole house erupted. With paws in the air, howling ensued.

"Who goes first?" Grey inquired.

"No particular order," Lane advised. "It's a free-for-all. George usually jumps onstage first since he's the chairman of the board. He thinks it's important that the residents see him involved. He'll just honk on the goose for a sec."

"Wait, what?" Grey asked. "What does that even mean?"

"That's what George calls his harmonica," Lane said, laughing. "The goose. It technically belongs to his human, Mr. Hughes. George taught himself how to play it. George will honk on the goose for a few minutes. Then he'll turn the microphone over to whoever wants to go next."

In a million years, Grey wouldn't have thought of George as a musician. She knew he was smart, but she had no idea there was a softer side to him. Grey couldn't believe it when George sat down on the stage, smiled at the crowd, and began to blow the beautiful, shiny instrument.

"Let's go after him," Grey suggested. "Then we can just hang out and chill for the rest of the night."

"Sounds good," Lane agreed.

Grey watched George deliver a three-minute acoustic performance called Moonlight. Grey could tell that George was transported to a place that was special to him. What a different perspective of the normally private Shepherd!

Grey jumped up as soon as George finished his song. She stepped onto the stage and studied the room. As Grey waited for Lane to get situated, she noticed that the kitchen cabinets were all open, and the pantry was ready to perform backup as needed. Grey also saw that George, Blaze, Meg, and Olivia were posing for a picture at the front door.

Grey thought about the last time she'd left her heart on the stage. She'd been terrified that she wouldn't know what to say. She'd learned that words mold in the moment. At the farm, she was the barn cat with the big voice. She was nervous that her song might sound different coming from the smallest fish in the city pond. Grey closed her eyes and waited for Lane to tap his empty jars. Grey met Lane's beat at the crossroads of her barn-life past and their pantry-filled present:

Another day, another time stamp, so be kind.
Another song, another chance to hit rewind.
Another friend, another reason to unwind.
Another stage, another spotlight we will mind.

The bet on life's big moments,
The minutes of your life,
The music of your memories,
The frames that you will find.

Let's sing to barn burners and empty jam jars too.
Let's mix it up the way that Argos mixers do.
Let's find a place for all animals to thrive.
Let's join the club where we get to feel alive.

I'm here to play the game of life,
so read my cards aloud.
We'll race to find out what they're all about.

· · · · · · · ·

Grey steered Lane through the crowd. She was dying to have her fortune read by Olivia. Grey knew it wasn't exactly Olivia's strong suit, but she didn't care. Grey walked straight to Olivia's table and was surprised to see that Olivia wasn't there.

"Let's find George," Lane offered. "George will know where Olivia is."

Together, Grey and Lane raced from room to room. They moved through the entire house. Strangely, none of the board members were present. George, Blaze, Meg, Mikey, and Olivia—all were missing at their own party.

"I saw some of the group pose for a picture by the front door as we stepped onto the stage," Grey remembered. "Did you notice that? Maybe they stepped outside to get a better photo."

Lane opened the front door to find Moosey in the middle of a ballet sequence. Moosey pointed his toe, raised his arms to arch above his head, and twirled around in a full circle before stepping back to take a deep bow.

"Don't worry, I'm here all night," Moosey assured them. "There's more where that came from."

"Have you seen George?" Lane asked. "Or any of the board members? Did they leave the party together?"

"Nope," Moosey answered.

Grey sensed by his wrinkled forehead that Moosey wasn't finished.

"Just the event crew leader," Moosey continued. "He said he was taking a load down to the dock. He had the big cart on wheels. He was very polite and timed it perfectly. He told me he didn't want to disturb any of the performances. He took the freight elevator."

Grey felt the front door open behind her at the exact moment Moosey wrapped up his report. Grey and Lane cocked their heads in unison to see who was standing in the doorway.

"Mikey!" Lane shouted in disbelief. "Man, am I glad to see you!"

"Sorry, dude," Mikey greeted. "I've been outside on the patio. I took a breather and forgot the board photo. Is Olivia mad? Where is she?"

"Olivia's missing," Lane replied. "With the exception of you, the entire board has disappeared."

"Let's stop and think about this," Grey suggested. "Why don't we go back to our house? There's bound to be something we're missing."

"Moosey, will you hang here in case they come back?" Lane requested.

"Roger that," Moosey replied. "No one's tapping in or out on my watch."

Grey turned toward her house. Lane and Mikey followed, but no one said a word. The silence was deafening, the weight of the moment marked by a Bernese bouncer who couldn't skirt the question of a potential security breach.

Grey had a bad feeling that this burner had just blazed out of control.

21

THROW ME A BONE

Lane paced the room. How had this happened? It made no sense whatsoever. They needed to retrace the entire day.

"We're overlooking something obvious," Lane insisted. "Board members don't disappear in a high-rise building . . . in a city . . . in the middle of a party."

"We started our day on the trails," Grey replied. "We went for a walk with Anne. Let's start there. What can we reasonably assume happened with the *other* board members this morning before the mixer?"

Lane saw Grey look to Mikey for guidance.

"Olivia has been in party planning mode all week," Mikey offered. "I ran into her yesterday. She was planning to have her event crew deliver a cart of party supplies. She was going to hide the crew in the maintenance closet overnight. She said that it was the only way she could guarantee that everything would be ready on time. She didn't want there to be a single hiccup in having the party setup completed first thing this morning."

"Wait a minute," Lane interrupted. "Are you telling me Olivia hid nonresident animals in the maintenance closet, on our floor, overnight? That's very unlike Olivia. She's normally so cautious."

"Well, we also know George would have walked the building this morning," Grey continued. "George walks the building every day. . . ."

"What is it?" Lane saw a look cross Grey's face.

"George walked the building!" Grey shrieked. "Then he stopped to see Crown, but Crown didn't answer the door. George brought an envelope for Crown. He left it here to keep it safe during the party. He made a point of telling me to remember that the envelope was under Stan's ottoman. It's in *this* room! He was telling me something important, and I didn't even realize it!"

Lane leapt through the air like someone had just thrown him a bone. Lane grabbed the envelope before Grey and Mikey could even blink. Lane read the message on the outside and gasped. He then ripped the envelope open to find a folder inside.

"George wrote, 'They're coming' on the outside of the envelope," Lane reported. "Then he wrote, 'Go to Crown' on the folder."

Lane pulled at the folder's contents.

"Those are the board meeting minutes," Mikey remarked. "We call the notes 'minutes.' You guys know that Crown is the official secretary of the board, so he usually takes the minutes and writes down everything said in the meeting. George has been doing it in his absence.

"But wait . . . this doesn't make any sense. George is a perfectionist. Everything always has to be just right. He's very serious about it. These notes have scribble marks and symbols all over the page. I can't make sense of this. These aren't just the meeting notes."

Lane heard the concern in Mikey's voice. He felt it too.

"Crown will know how to read them," Lane replied. "Crown can read just about anything."

CHAPTER TWENTY-TWO

CROWNING ACHIEVEMENT

C rown was born in another state, in every sense of the word.

Crown's first owner, Kenny, had been a gambler. Kenny gambled on everything. Crown knew Kenny loved cards the most. Over the years, Crown learned that possessions meant very little to Kenny. Kenny had lots of them, and he won or lost on a whim without ever bothering to size up his surroundings.

Crown took a different approach. He read the room like the back of his paw. He knew how humans and animals would react to a situation before they did. Crown had watched Kenny cheat, lie, and then cheat some more. Crown recognized that Kenny wasn't loyal to anyone or anything.

Crown would never forget the day Willy appeared at Kenny's weekend cabin for game night. Willy was a free spirit and a wanderer with hair all the way down his back. He was the friend of a friend who showed up for a single night. It was the night that would change Crown's entire life.

Crown saw Willy enter the room. Willy immediately walked toward their table. He seemed light as a feather, as though floating through air. Crown looked straight ahead while Willy sat down in the chair beside Kenny. At first, Willy was loose and likeable, but that wasn't what caught Crown's attention. Like Crown, Willy appeared to be watching the room. Willy participated in conversations without giving anything away. Not about his cards, and certainly not about himself. Hours passed like minutes. Out of nowhere, Crown felt the focus of Willy's stare turn to him. Then, time stood still.

"That your dog?" Willy asked.

"Sure is," Kenny replied. "I've got a few, but this one was born out here on the land. That your Silver Bullet?"

Crown watched Kenny point to the silver trailer parked in front of the cabin.

"Sure is," Willy replied. "I've had her for years. Her name is Grace. I've driven across the country with her, coast to coast. I was surprised that you didn't have a similar ride sitting outside already."

"I've thought about getting a trailer for years," Kenny acknowledged. "I've got just about everything else you could think of. Tell me, what's she worth to you?" Kenny smiled.

"Grace?" Willy laughed. "Grace isn't for sale."

"Come on," Kenny nudged. "There's got to be something you'd consider trading her for."

Crown could tell that Willy thought very little of Kenny. Crown also knew that Kenny hadn't figured that out for himself yet.

"Do you bet on everything?" Willy asked.

"You bet," Kenny replied, excited by the direction the conversation was taking.

"How about that dog?" Willy inquired. "What's he worth to you?"

"You want to play a Cavalier King Charles Spaniel for a Silver Bullet?" Kenny asked, laughing. "Deal me in."

"Not exactly," Willy replied as he leaned over to pick up Crown. "You're going to deal. You'll play against the dog. If the dog barks, we'll take another card. If the dog remains quiet, we'll hold. No new cards. If the dog wins, he goes with me, and we'll ride away with Grace. If the dog loses, I'll leave alone and on foot."

"Why would you do that?" Kenny asked.

"Because you need to count your blessings for a change," Willy answered. "All I've seen you count is cards. You can't cheat your way through life. No one wins, including you. I'm sure the dog has watched it too. I'm sure he's seen you count your crowning achievements on one hand. I'm betting he's seen you fold them all too.

"I'm not a gambler myself. I earned Grace. I'm grateful for the road I've traveled with her. I've learned to walk away when it's time. I just don't see myself having to walk anywhere tonight. I'll guide the dog through the game. Then I suspect I'll drive us home."

Crown sat comfortably in Willy's lap. He was ready for his road trip.

. . . .

Crown answered the door on the first knock.

"The board is missing!" Lane barked. "We know George stopped by here earlier today. He wanted to give you his most recent HOA board meeting notes. George told Grey that you weren't home, so he left the folder in our study. We went to the mixer together, and then halfway through the party, the board disappeared. We think George knew that something bad was about to happen, but we can't figure out what his notes mean. We just know that he wanted us to bring them to you for help. He literally wrote the words 'Go to Crown.'"

Crown motioned for the group to follow him inside. Crown took a deep breath and accepted the folder from Lane. He then began laying the sheets of paper on the dining room table. Crown made sure to put the paper in a specific order.

"George would have placed the oldest papers on the top," Crown instructed. "He'd tell you the tale from start to finish, top to bottom, and expect you to experience the entire story. We'll have to read it in the correct order to know if, how, and where George wants us to step in. That's the only way to figure out what's going on."

Crown made three neat rows of paper. Each row contained five sheets. Crown started with the cover letter from the previous board meeting. He placed it on the top row on the left side.

"I was in that meeting," Mikey noted. "I remember what we talked about. It's all here. What did George hear that I didn't? What did I miss?"

Crown silently studied the first page. He saw that George had begun to make notes in the margin. Crown had a hunch those notes were intended for him.

"Look at this," Crown instructed. "George wrote, 'Blaze dropping brochures. What will they say? Watch for them.'"

Crown waited for a reaction.

"George saw this whole thing playing out weeks ago!" Grey shouted as she paced the room. "But what's so special about the brochures? What could they possibly have to do with this?"

"Hold up," Lane instructed. "Blaze made the brochures, and now Blaze is gone. That's a little too convenient. Is Blaze behind the board disappearance?"

"We don't know that yet," Crown replied. "Let's not jump to any conclusions. We're just getting started here. Look at page ten. George also wrote, 'Olivia's setup.' Does he mean setting up the party?"

Crown flipped another page over and saw the next clue. He knew they were getting close.

"George walks the building every day," Crown reminded them.

"I totally said that same exact thing right before we came here!" Grey exclaimed.

"Well, look at this," Crown continued. "George made a note that there are lights out on the first floor in the stairwell. That's a security flag. If the lights are out, you can't see who's coming or going. It's too dark by the back exit."

"What's in the circle?" Mikey pointed to a circle above the note about the lights.

"That says 'SEAL,'" Grey read aloud. "Seal to what, though? Is George talking about the seal to the door? I've never noticed any problem with it before."

Crown read the last sheet of paper. It appeared to be Blaze's Argos flyer with pictures drawn all over it.

"This must be a copy of the brochure Blaze dropped on the Trinity Trails," Crown concluded. He flipped the page over and abruptly stopped.

"What is it?" Grey demanded.

Crown saw the note from George. Crown knew with total certainty that George had outlined exactly what to do next. He also knew that none of them would have any idea what the note meant. It appeared to be written in a special, scribbled code. It looked as though George had written these final thoughts in a matter of seconds.

"Let's piece the clues together," Crown suggested. "Perhaps the answer to the code is lurking by the lights. Why else would George have written these two things together? We need to see the stairwell as George saw it."

Crown stood slowly, still shaky on his feet.

"I can't tell you what this clue means," Crown continued. "But I feel certain that the stairwell can. We'll find the answers on the first floor. We can count on that."

Count your blessings.

23

CHAPTER TWENTY-THREE
HEADS OF STATE

Polly watched Mi and Co wipe their foreheads. She could see that they were both dripping in sweat. Still, Mi and Co managed to smile in her direction as they high-fived each member of their crew.

As the heads of the Doubt Detector Star Department, Mi and Co had gathered a team of eleven rising stars to assist with the dog's state of mind. The team of thirteen had formed a strategic circle around the room. Each star remained hidden and out of sight to the animal below. The stars' suits helped them blend into the stark, bare walls of the small space.

Polly knew it had taken every tool in their toolbox to beat doubt today. Fortunately, the stars were equipped with white arrows that hung on their backs, as well as cloud puffs they kept in their pockets. The cloud puffs blew away destructive ideas before they had a chance to stick. The stars had been forced to fight layer upon layer of insecurity, and the first doubt appeared as soon as the dog sat down. The stars watched the thought bubble form immediately.

You don't have what it takes to go the distance, the dog said to himself.

Star #3 shot an arrow before the bubble could move into the dog's mind.

You're not strong enough, the dog insisted.

Star #7 pulled his puff and shot the insecurity away.

Thought after thought appeared in bubbles beside this dog. The Doubt Detectors prevailed. All of the dog's self-destructive words had been destroyed. The unorganized and defeated letters raced away as fast as they could.

Polly knew it was now time to plant the seed for joy.

CHAPTER TWENTY-FOUR
SCOUT

L ane carried Crown down the Argos stairs on his
back. He then led his friend through the back
hallway on the first floor. Grey and Mikey followed behind.

"Stop if you hear anything," Crown whispered to
Lane.

Lane nodded and understood that whatever they

were up against might make his ears zing. Lane walked steadily with his head down.

A voice emerged. "We were a team, you and me," the voice said. "I want to make you proud."

Lane gently nudged Crown to stop. Seconds after hearing the voice, Lane saw the dark shadow of a sunken Retriever in the stairwell. Based on what Lane could see and hear, Lane assumed the dog was a shell of his normal self. The dog's ears dragged on the ground, and his eyes stared straight ahead at the wall.

Lane watched the dog's body react as it sensed their presence. Lane could tell that even in the Retriever's reduced state, his reflexes were superior. The dog's muscles bulged.

"We're not here to bother you," Lane began slowly. "My name is Lane. This is Crown, Grey, and Mikey."

"What do you want?" the worn-down dog barked.

"We think our friends have just been kidnapped," Lane continued. "One of them left clues behind in a folder. The clues are written in some kind of code. We suspect that the clue is tied to a search and rescue mission written by a smart German Shepherd. It looks like the Shepherd had a hunch something terrible was about to happen. He mapped out a plan before he even needed one. The problem is that we don't know how to read it. One of the clues pointed us to the lights in the stairwell. The Shepherd also wrote the word *SEAL* and circled it. The circle was next to the note about the lights. You're sitting in the exact spot the Shepherd circled. That's why we're here."

Lane watched the dog's demeanor change. The dog began grinding his jaw back and forth. Lane noticed the dog's vest was the same blue color as Blaze's faux sheriff costume. The vest also had a red, white, and blue oval-shaped patch with a white star and the number "1" written in yellow.

Is this a setup? the dog wondered silently to himself.

Lane's ears shot up as he studied the dog intently. Something very profound had happened to this animal.

"I can read the code," the dog finally replied aloud. "I'm a Golden Retriever, trained for search and rescue. I can find your friends. Show me the folder."

"What's your name?" Grey asked.

The dog stared each of them squarely in the eye. Lane saw pride return to the dog's stature. Lane noted that the dog's eyes no longer looked sad. His ears no longer dragged. The dog stood tall.

"My name is Scout," the dog declared.

Lane had a hunch this dog had risked it all to rescue many.

"Follow us," Lane directed.

Lane led the way, as he propped Crown on his back to carry him back up the stairs. Scout and the group followed closely behind.

Lane had no doubt that Scout could help them search, rescue, and perhaps even battle whoever had taken their board members. However, Lane also sensed that Scout was on a search of his own. Lane wondered how and where the dog had gotten so lost.

25

CHAPTER TWENTY-FIVE
UNLEASHED EVENTS

Grey watched Scout comb through every single word of George's notes.

"George scribbled the first note beside Blaze's offer to distribute brochures," Scout noticed. "Was her offer out of character?"

"Yes, it was," Grey replied.

"OK, let's assume George was on to Blaze," Scout continued. "Perhaps George sensed that Blaze was using this opportunity to send a message to someone. Blaze said 'brochures.' That means she managed to drop at least one brochure since this was left behind. Let's look at what Blaze wrote on the brochure. We need to compare it with what George scribbled. George somehow read between the lines. We'll have to do the same."

"I've been thinking about that as well," Crown offered. "Blaze included information about the building, the board, the mixer . . . even today's date. Blaze broadcast the fact that the Argos animals were all getting together. She compromised the safety of the building and the board. Blaze also knew that Olivia was bringing in an event crew to set up the stage. All someone had to do was put the pieces together to target the board."

"An organized group would probably map out one of two possible plans," Scout agreed. "Either they came in the event crew's place, or they staged a takeover when the crew arrived. The question is: Who would have seen this brochure on the trails and had anything to gain from the Argos animals?"

"All I can think is the strays," Crown offered.

"Who are the strays?" Scout asked.

"The strays are a group of animals that live on the Trinity Trails," Grey explained. Even she could hear the bite in her voice. "Why are you jumping to that conclusion, Crown?"

"I can't think of anyone else," Crown confessed.

"What do the strays have to gain?" Scout asked.

"I don't know yet," Crown replied. "Perhaps we'll find those answers next."

"Let's assume the strays are behind this," Scout replied. "They would have needed a way to enter the building without being seen. That's probably where George wrote his code. Three dots, followed by three dashes, followed by three dots is Morse code."

"Morse what?" Mikey asked.

"Morse code," Scout said. "It's an old code used to communicate. The code was a method to send messages back and forth. I know this because I've been trained to know it as a reference point in rescue operations. You never know what you could be up against. I'm not sure how George would know it, though. What does George's human do for a living?"

"Mr. Hughes is a retired detective," Lane acknowledged.

"Based on what I've seen so far, I'd guess that Mr. Hughes has a set of history books, and George has a sense of humor. But Morse code is no joke. It's an SOS emergency code."

"What does SOS stand for?" Grey asked.

"Save Our Ship," Scout answered.

"What do the dots and dashes mean?" Grey continued.

"That reads 21M," Scout replied.

"That's the maintenance closet!" Mikey screamed. "The Argos maintenance closet is on the twenty-first floor. It's 21M!"

"If the strays staged a takeover, that's where we'll find the event crew that was left behind," Crown concluded.

Grey felt a quiet rage erupt inside of her. She couldn't understand why it was always so easy for her friends to assume the worst of other animals.

. . . .

Grey stared at the numbers: 21M. She had been in this very closet, two days prior, to remove the rope for her costume. It felt like a lifetime ago.

Grey saw Lane and Scout motion for her to let them enter first. She nodded her head to confirm. She didn't know how bad the situation was going to be inside that room. Grey was grateful for their offer to go ahead.

Grey watched Scout make a high-low dart move to break inside the room. She had never seen anything like it. Lane followed and quickly shut the door behind them. Grey, Mikey, and Crown stood together in silence. They waited for a sign, any sign. The door finally opened.

"It's dark in there," Lane reported. "The lights are now out in this room, too. We're looking for a flashlight. Watch your step and stand by me."

The maintenance room was filled with materials for the building: extra doors, appliances, saws, and brooms. Shelves were stocked with paint, brushes, tools, and gloves. Grey could see the outline of three animals against the far wall. She squinted to let her eyes adjust, and then the whole picture became clear. She had no idea what to expect, but it certainly wasn't an orange tabby cat, a Bluetick Coonhound, and a green lizard. All three animals were trapped under the paint shelves. Their forelegs had been tied behind them.

"Don't hurt us," the lizard begged.

"You're safe now," Lane assured. "Let us untie you. Then tell us what happened."

Grey watched Scout slowly approach the terrified threesome. Scout cut the ties around their wrists.

"We work the buildings in the neighborhood," the tabby explained. "If an animal wants to throw a party, we're the event team that makes it happen. We're called the 'Unleashed Events.' We know which shops have the best flowers and food, and we follow their schedules. We pull the inventory as it's needed. Olivia uses us to manage big parties."

"I have the best nose in town," the Coonhound continued. "I can track down anything. We knew this event would be an overnight job, so we made special arrangements. We have a large, enclosed cart that we use to carry around items. We loaded the flowers and the decorations, but we didn't notice that there was a cat hiding in the cart. Olivia opened the back door to the building to let us inside. She led us to this room and made sure we were in place for the night. The moment Olivia left the room, the cat jumped out and tied us up. He moved so fast we didn't even realize what was happening. At least, not until it was too late."

"In case you're wondering, I'm the insurance policy on the team," the lizard explained. "My fellow reptile family won't stand for one of their kind getting harmed. The Trinity Trails creek moccasins will make it their mission to find the animal that did this to me. They will bring justice for me. For *us*." The lizard looked at his team.

"Do you know who it was?" Lane asked. "Did you see the cat's face?"

"Davy the Stray did this," the lizard said, seething with anger.

Grey felt Lane's eyes pierce through her patterned fur.

"Looks like we reached that fork in the road," Lane whispered. "I assume this has unleashed any misguided loyalty you once felt."

Grey closed her eyes. She could feel her soul sink.

26

CHAPTER TWENTY-SIX
STRAYS ON SITE

Davy had watched Willow fall asleep. He noticed that Willow seemed unusually at peace. It almost looked to Davy as though Willow had found an answer and was resting at ease. He wondered what the question had been. That question nagged at him all night.

As the morning sun began to flicker, Davy saw that something had changed. Willow wasn't moving or breathing. He pushed and poked, but Willow didn't respond. It suddenly dawned on Davy that Willow had gone to sleep for the sole purpose of joining her beloved husband in her dreams. Willow had finally made it to their shared hallway.

Davy didn't know what to do next, or what it meant for him. His first thought was to run. He leapt like lightning through the cat door and across the yard. Davy heard Berma shouting in the distance, but he couldn't stop to explain. His mind raced to keep up with his body. Davy arrived at Jojo's front door. He screamed. He yelled for the heartache he felt in a sunrise he'd never forget. He watched as the lights flickered inside the house. The doorknob turned. Jojo opened the door and looked down. Davy watched their shared reality settle into Jojo's face. Then Jojo began to run too.

The days that followed went by in a blur. Davy found solace under Berma's seat. He hid from the blend of relatives and friends that appeared to pay their respects. Finally, after the last of the guests left, the quiet question of Davy's future resurfaced. Davy slowly walked up the hill to the house. He made it halfway through the yard before a young man emerged.

Davy recognized the young man immediately. It was Willow's son, Kyle. Kyle looked tired and sad. Both emotions were understandable. Davy hadn't officially met Kyle, but he'd heard stories and seen photos. Kyle had been Willow's favorite, though she'd never admit it to anyone other than Davy.

"There's a stray in the yard!" Kyle yelled.

Davy guessed Kyle was speaking to whomever else remained in the house. Davy was confused. He had never heard the word *stray* and wondered what Kyle meant.

"Get rid of it," a young woman's voice yelled. "We can't have random cats roaming around the yard if we're planning to sell the house."

Davy watched Kyle grab a stick and shake it in his direction.

"Scat, cat," Kyle shouted. "And don't bring any of your other stray friends around here either. This is not your home. We'll call the pound to pick you up."

Davy stood very still as his world began to spin. He watched the door close. Davy was left with nothing but the memory of a life that had disappeared. He turned and walked toward the creek. He wondered if this life had ever really existed in the first place. Had he always been a stray? Or had he suddenly become one? What did it mean to become a stray? Davy hadn't changed, but clearly the perception of him had. Was that really all it took to deny him his home?

Davy watched the doorway to his dignity shut, but he knew that he was not alone. Kyle had mentioned "friends." Davy intended to find them.

· · · · · · · ·

Davy walked past Berma without missing a beat. He grabbed a stick of his own and jumped back into the water. The same water that had carried Davy to the white house on the hill would now return him to the life he thought he escaped. The construction on the creek had been completed. The swim was less demanding than it had been before. Davy kicked his hind legs, and the current carried him safely to the other side.

Davy yanked at the stones on the shoreline. He sat beside the newly placed drainage pipe and closed his eyes to think about everything that had happened. Davy had loved and lost Willow. He wondered if love and loss always overlapped. He felt the sting of tears stain his already filthy face.

Davy found comfort in knowing that he was not alone. Kyle said there were others like him. Perhaps they had been separated from loved ones. Perhaps they had lost their way. Maybe there were others whose situation left them scrambling to make sense of it all too. Davy knew he was a natural listener and a born leader. He could create a community among the animals. This wasn't just about him. Davy needed to establish a space for all of the Trinity Trails strays to thrive.

Davy spent weeks envisioning a plan. He focused on building his foundation first. He couldn't risk it falling apart like before. He called it ground zero. Davy searched the old construction spots along the creek for materials that had been left behind. He found everything he needed. The days were long, and the nights were hard. He ground his grief into the walls he built around him. The walls would protect him. They needed to be sturdy but inviting. The walls weren't there to keep other animals out. They were there to keep the fear of failure away. Fear was noisy. Davy hoped the quiet would give courage a chance to speak up instead.

The creek construction had installed a new set of stairs next to the updated drainage pipes. The metal stairs extended all the way down to the creek. Davy built his house safely underneath the stairs and used gravel to camouflage the outline of the home, from the grass to the creek's edge. Mossy wood framed the house, and Davy found discarded metal sheets to form a makeshift roof. The gravel provided a steady ground so the wood could stand tall. The wood worked to hold up the metal roof. Together, all of the materials collaborated to create something whose sum total was bigger than the individual parts.

Davy thought about what to name the newly built home. He used chalk that he'd found on a morning walk to write the letters *SOS* on the front door. Davy smiled at his personal victory. He'd worked hard for this home, and he intended to share it.

"Strays on Site," Davy said with a laugh as he stared at the letters. "And for the animals that need to stay a while, we'll call it Camp David."

. . . .

Davy's porch quickly became his new favorite spot. As the day faded to dusk and the moon began to glow, the Trinity Trails "Creek Quartet" delighted the creek residents with melodies from the drainpipe. Davy relished the fact that he had a front row seat.

The quartet consisted of a cricket, a cardinal, a moccasin, and a beaver. The beaver was a natural-born performer. He shook a tambourine from the top of the song each time. The cricket's chirps hung in the air like a throaty clarinet, punching the song's pulse over the water's waves. As talented as they were, the beaver and cricket were still no match for the cardinal, whose voice carried hope and harmony. The music offered comfort to the creek. Animals listened and watched as the park lights flickered on.

Davy had spent weeks assembling the parts for his house. He looked around his porch with pride. The house was built to blend in. The gravel created the illusion of a continuation of the creek. Most importantly, the grayish-blue water matched the metal roof, which also matched the metal stairs. Anyone looking down at Davy's home would have a hard time finding it.

Davy was proud of the work he'd put into his home. He was even prouder of the work he'd put into himself. He thought a lot about the word *stray*. What did it really mean to be a *stray*? Davy had loved Willow with his whole heart. Davy knew he was supposed to meet Willow. He also knew he wasn't supposed to stay with her. Davy realized that the real test had been in his ability to move "forward," just like the missing cross-word in Willow's puzzle.

Davy began to think that being a stray was a good thing. It was a compliment. It didn't mean he was alone or below the bar set by other animals. He didn't have to be reduced by someone else's definition of what a house cat should be. Becoming a stray simply meant that he'd separated from the status quo. Davy could begin to think differently. He could think for himself and help other animals do the same. Perhaps the word *stray* would stand for those who had risen above judgment. Davy was deep in thought when his first new friend appeared.

"Is this place safe?" a tired-looking, red-eared turtle asked as he slowly approached.

"You have no idea just how safe this spot is," Davy declared. "Can I help you?"

"I need to rest," the turtle replied. "It's been a long road getting here."

"Welcome to the club," Davy said with a smile.

CHAPTER TWENTY-SEVEN

WINGMAN

Davy wiped the tears of laughter from his face. Rand the Red-Eared Turtle had been talking for hours about his many encounters with birds. Who knew that turtles were secretly bird-watchers?

Davy learned that Rand was an old turtle. Rand had been around a long time, and he had the lines to show for it. Deeply embedded, beautiful streaks of green and yellow and lime covered his entire body, from his arms to his legs, his stomach to his shell, and even the creases around his eyes. The streaks backed right up to his red "ears," which weren't actually ears at all. They were bright red spots where ears should have been. Davy found it hysterical that the red spots grew brighter and brighter as the good part of Rand's tale drew near.

Davy discovered that Rand's favorite stories revolved around a particularly feisty pelican. Davy was dying to hear how the pelican's story ended.

"What finally happened?" Davy asked.

"She told me Louisiana was the pelican state," Rand acknowledged. "And off she went."

"How long did she stay?" Davy inquired.

"Three seasons," Rand answered.

"Then she returned?" Davy whispered.

"Like no time had passed," Rand responded.

"Was it complicated when she came back?" Davy asked. "Her friends must have moved on. I bet the beach wasn't the same as when she left it. Was it weird for the pelican?"

"Nope," Rand replied. "The pelican left all of her baggage behind. She was light as a feather when she flew back. She returned happy, and happiness spreads.

The other birds learned from the pelican's experience. They soaked up her joy and benefitted from her journey. Even I learned a lesson or two about starting fresh."

"I should say," Davy joked. "You appear to be traveling light."

"I have everything I need," Rand confirmed.

"You don't want anything else?" Davy asked. "Come on, everyone wants something."

"I'm talking about needs, not wants," Rand clarified. "They're totally different things. Take the pelican. She was a funny bird. She knew who she was at her core. She called it her 'suitcase.' The pelican said that over time she had filled her suitcase with what she thought she *wanted*. But when she added real-life experiences to the bag, it became too heavy to carry around. She couldn't fly with all that extra weight. So she decided to spend some time cleaning out her suitcase to make room for what she actually *needed* in her heart and soul.

"The pelican went somewhere safe to 'unpack.' She called it 'the pelican state' for laughs. One day, she felt lighter and true to herself. That's when she returned, just as she promised she would. The pelican taught me that life only gets complicated when you keep your suitcase filled with stuff you no longer need. That's when you make things harder than they have to be.

In the end, the pelican felt strong enough to lead her own fleet and fly on her own terms. That's called clean living. Carry only what continues to serve you."

Davy watched Rand retract his arms and legs inside his shell.

"You know they're coming, right?" Rand asked.

"I wouldn't have it any other way." Davy smiled as he stared at the path ahead.

*Carry only
what continues
to serve you.*

28

CHAPTER TWENTY-EIGHT

THE POWER OF SHARING

Grey had been sitting in the living room for an hour. It was darker than normal. Colder too. Lane had closed the curtains in a paranoid attempt at privacy. Not even the sun could shine light on this disaster of a day.

Grey tried her best to stay calm as Lane and Mikey quizzed the new members of their team. Grey's eyes darted from the Bluetick Coonhound to the tabby cat and then to the lizard. Grey had learned that the cat was named Connie, the Bluetick Coonhound was named Betsy, and the lizard was actually a gecko named Gage.

Grey was now focused solely on Scout. Grey noticed that Scout's body language was completely different than the dog they had met just hours earlier. Scout seemed steady and strong, with his ears on high alert.

"We may not be the group that George had in mind," Scout began. "However, we collectively represent the best chance for the board to return home. This is a search and rescue mission. We will each need to bring forth special skills. Some groups in my past called them 'special forces.' Why don't we take a minute and figure out what we have to work with as a team?"

Grey's eyes darted once more, this time from Crown to Lane.

"What is it?" Scout asked.

"Connie, Betsy, and Gage . . . would you guys wait in the bedroom for a second?" Crown asked. "We need to speak privately, but I promise it will only take a moment."

Grey grinned to herself. She knew this was about to get real. Grey watched the threesome walk to the bedroom. She noticed that they looked relieved to have time to themselves. Grey didn't blame them. The sound of Crown clearing his throat brought her back to the situation at hand.

"Well?" Scout asked.

"Open the drapes," Grey demanded. She waited for her words to do their work. The words created a hook to gently carry the shocked fabric from one side of the window to the other. Grey watched as Scout, Lane, and Crown squinted in the newly lit room. Grey let out a deep sigh, grateful to the curtains for being agreeable for once.

"Show off!" Lane laughed.

"Stripes?" Mikey mouthed.

Grey gathered that Mikey was minutes away from an epic freak-out.

"Grey's got the pipes, but I've got the drums," Lane bragged as he stood up. "Meaning, she has a magic voice, but I have magic ears."

"Is this a dream?" Mikey demanded. "I'm dreaming, right?"

"Eardrums," Lane insisted. "Magic ears . . . eardrums. I can hear the inner thoughts of animals in need of help. That doesn't mean I hear everything. My 'special force' only works if I'm supposed to assist. If I can help an animal in some way, I can hear the voice in their head. I was born this way. So was Grey."

"Can you *hear* how crazy you sound?" Mikey insisted.

"This just gets better and better," Scout scoffed.

"My words can take any shape," Grey explained. "As you just saw, they can even fly. I have to use them selectively, though. If I give an order, they will fulfill it. So, yes, like Lane's ears, they only work with good intention."

Grey knew that Mikey was on the verge of a meltdown. She could see time ticking on down his face. However, Crown was as cool as a cucumber. In fact, Grey sensed that Crown wasn't stressed about anything. In light of the circumstances, she found that notably odd.

"Why didn't you tell me this before?" Mikey asked. "I'm clearly the last to know."

"It wasn't about you," Grey replied.

"Animals get paranoid when they know," Lane added.

Grey shot Lane a look of annoyance.

"That isn't it either," Grey continued. "I fuel the confidence behind my words. It's got to be my energy, not yours or anyone else's. I prioritize my voice, and its potential, over other animals' pride. This is about my responsibility to me and to the difference I can make for others. That takes precedence."

"I respect that," Mikey said, marveling. "I get it. But now I feel like I'm the one falling short on this team."

Grey watched Mikey remove his glasses to stare squarely at each of them. For the very first time, Grey saw that Mikey's eyes were large, wide-set, and bright blue, like hers.

"Look, I've got a good gut sense," Mikey continued. "I *usually* don't miss details. I see things that others overlook, and I can find treasure in trash. I'll tell you if the juice is worth the squeeze, but I certainly wouldn't consider that a 'special power.' I'm not qualified to be part of this group."

"You see things that others overlook," Grey repeated.

"That's what he said," Scout stated. "Qualified or not, you're here. I think we need to focus on Davy, anyway. We have a lot of unanswered questions. Why Davy would do this in the first place? What can the board do for him? Does anyone know Davy's story?"

"His human died," Mikey replied. "The word on the creek is that Davy's owner was an old woman. She took Davy in, and they became inseparable. Then one day, she had a sudden heart attack in her sleep. I'm not sure what happened to Davy after that. I think we can all assume that it must have been very traumatic. I'm sure whatever we're up against lies in that quiet grief."

"We'll have to see the world through Davy's eyes to understand what's driving his decisions," Grey agreed as she walked to the window with the open drapes.

· · · · · · · ·

Grey stood at the window and closed her eyes.

"You told me to call on you when I need you," Grey whispered. "It's funny how hard it is to ask for help. It shouldn't be. It's such a simple thing.

"We need to see life as Davy does. We need to know what it was like for him to become a stray. It's our only chance of connecting. It's also the only way the Argos animals can understand the choices Davy has had to make. They'll be forced to relate to Davy in order to rescue the board. That kind of vision comes from a higher source.

"Please share your light to guide us along our path. Please magnify Mikey's gift so we can see what's important. I fear that *this* is the fork in the road. I'm not sure which direction is really right, but I know I'll need help turning the wheel either way."

Grey suddenly sensed a presence and knew she wasn't alone. Her chest had a sudden chill, and her fur stood at attention. Then it felt like a warm blanket had wrapped itself around her whole body.

Grey knew that her friend Bo the Wise Owl was with her. Bo had just given Mikey the special force he would need for this mission. Mikey's new gift would allow him to see Davy the way Davy deserved to be seen. Grey turned and walked back to the table.

"Mikey, there's something I need to tell you," Grey began.

29

CHAPTER TWENTY-NINE

THE AMAZING RACE

"So, this is what the short straw looks like," Scout concluded, his voice dripping in sarcasm.

Scout stared at Lane, Grey, and Mikey. Scout had heard a lot of things in his life. He'd seen a lot of things too. Scout had been trained to succeed under extreme stress, and pressure didn't bother him. The more intense the situation, the better he'd always performed.

Even still, nothing could have prepared Scout for this moment. The moment his team would consist of a barn cat with a magic voice, a Lab with magic ears, and a longhair cat with all-seeing glasses, whatever that meant. All of this to rescue a hodgepodge of fancy board animals that had been taken hostage by a stray cat named Davy.

"Tell me one more time," Mikey requested. "There's an owl named Bo. He wears glasses that can see everything—the past, present, and future? Where do I jump on the magic carpet ride to chat with your buddy Bo? Where does Bo live?"

"On a mountaintop," Grey said. "Bo's off the grid, and yes, he sees all. He can tune in to different frequencies, and his glasses help him zoom in to moments that need immediate attention. Bo helped me make sense of my journey. His glasses showed me the path to the Argos. Bo is going to guide *your* glasses so they detect whatever clue we need to uncover today."

"Mikey, do you see anything right now?" Scout asked.

"Nothing unusual," Mikey replied with concern.

"You won't," Grey clarified. "Bo will simply give you the tools you need when it's time. From there, we're all going to have to work together to understand what the clues mean. Things are rarely what they seem. We'll have to look below the surface to find the trigger that caused Davy to do what he did. There's always a trigger."

Scout paused and looked toward the bedroom. "We'll have to bring the gecko," he replied.

"Why?" Grey asked. "I have faith in what each of us brings to the table. We have all the skills that we need for this mission. I don't want to put anyone else in danger."

"That's where we differ," Scout answered. "I lost faith a while back. Plus, I've been trained to plan for any possible situation. We may need backup."

Scout could tell that Grey was taken aback. He stood and walked toward the bedroom. Scout gently tapped on the door and returned to his seat.

"I mean, really?" Gage squealed as he waved his arms in the air. "I've been stuck with these two since yesterday. How about a little team effort on the clock?"

"Go fish," Betsy bantered.

"Quit projecting." Gage grinned.

"Sorry, Gage." Grey laughed. "We were just talking about your safety net with the snakes. Can you confirm that all the Trinity Trails water moccasins have your back? I mean, what happens exactly?"

The group focused intently on Gage.

"You do realize that I can't lose a staring competition, right?" Gage mocked. "I literally can't blink. Choose your battles."

"Always with the blinking," Betsy countered with a smirk.

"Moving on," Gage continued. "The snakes consider me family. They've always made it clear that I can gauge a situation and take the appropriate risk. That's why they named me Gage. They'll do whatever it takes to protect me."

"Understood," Scout acknowledged. "We want you to join us today. This mission may involve the creek if I'm reading George's clues right. He called this a SEAL mission for a reason. I think we're going to have to deal with water at some point. I don't know when or where or how. It's just a feeling I have."

"To be clear, we don't think we're going to need you," Lane added. "But we'd feel better if we had the backup, just in case."

Scout could tell that Gage liked feeling important. Scout understood. He had worked really hard to feel important in life too.

"Betsy, I'd like for you to join us as well," Scout requested.

"Wait . . . what?" Lane leaned in and spoke with

urgency. "We need to keep the group small. It's getting too big. We'll be too visible."

"Actually, it's the opposite," Scout explained. "Gage and Betsy are going to go first. They will leave the Argos separately. Davy is waiting for something to happen. He knows that we will respond to a hostage situation. The Stray Club will stalk whoever goes first, and they can't touch Gage.

"Gage, your job will be to reach the moccasins. They'll likely have a role in this.

"Betsy, we'll need you to follow Gage. Sniff out the situation. Then find us on the trails.

"Going first, all eyes will be on both of you. Betsy is trained for it, and Gage is safe since the snakes are watching out for him. This should give us the time we need to figure out what's really going on.

"Lane, Grey, Mikey, and I will be exactly seven minutes behind Betsy. Those minutes will give us time to put the team's special skills to work. There will be six of us on the trails, and we'll all work together. Don't forget, this is a dance. Each move is choreographed and calculated. One misstep affects everyone involved. I guess you could say that we've just become Team 6: Special and Enhanced Animals . . . with a Lizard. So, there's our own version of a SEAL."

Gage cleared his throat.

"You know it works better with 'lizard,'" Scout said laughing.

"I know you need me on those trails," Gage retorted. "Call it what you want; I'm the first one out the door." Gage bowed and beckoned applause.

"What about us?" Connie asked. "Do Crown and I stay here at the Argos?"

"Yes," Scout confirmed. "You're the creative one, right? You can figure out how to make parties appear a certain way?"

"I can make a room look any way you want it to," Connie confirmed. "I can make it rain."

"That's what I thought," Scout said. "We need you to make sure that no one knows we're gone. Move things around. Take food out of the bowls. Do whatever you think is necessary to make the rooms look lived in. We need for it to seem like we've been here all afternoon."

"Brilliant," Lane barked. "And we'll bring back our board!" Lane banged his paws against the table.

Scout stood. He adjusted his vest and collected his thoughts, hoping to inspire the group and rally their courage.

"I've heard a lot of speeches in my day," Scout began. "If you'll do me the honor of gathering around, I'll lead you in what's called a 'rallying cry.' We can sing it together on the trails when we need to cheer one another on. Teams that work together like this often have songs to keep their spirits up on tough days.

"Sing along with me as you pick up on it:

The Argos Animals among us,
All together as one.
The Trails of Trinity to join us,
In step with the sun.

Honor those who came before us,
Bring them peace today.
Light the path ahead to guide us,
And watch out if you're a stray!

CHAPTER THRITY
THE SHORT LIST

Gage was the first to leave the Argos. His teammates pushed the back door open and patted him on the back. Gage was cool and collected. *Ready, set, go.* He counted the lines in the pavement as he skipped down the sidewalk.

Gage was the smallest member of Team 6. He was also the happiest to be heading to the creek. That hadn't always been the case. Gage thought about his early days as he approached the Trinity Trails gate.

Gage had been bullied as a baby gecko. The teasing started with the other lizards. Gage was the last one to have a growth spurt. Most just teased him about being small because his tail hadn't filled in yet. The vicious ones took it a step further. They nicknamed Gage "Invisa-Liz." They found every way to make him feel smaller than he was. Gage could handle the lizards. The real problem started when a daunting creek cat discovered him too.

Every day, Gage waited for Jesse the Joker to appear. In hindsight, Gage understood that none of the other cats on the creek liked Jesse either. They didn't agree with what Jesse was saying and doing to Gage. They were just scared to draw any attention to themselves. The other cats didn't want Jesse to turn on them too, so they stayed silent and watched. Day after day—until Jesse took it too far.

Jesse trapped Gage by holding his short tail down with his paw. Gage's legs reached for any way to escape. Gage used every ounce of inner strength to keep from crying. He shook violently, but he would not break.

Jesse was laughing so hard that he never saw Viper the Cottonmouth coming. Viper was the leader of the

Creek Water Moccasins and known for a zero-tolerance policy on pushing around his fellow reptiles. The reptiles were all family as far as Viper was concerned.

Viper's large black and brown body coiled and rose up. His triangular jaw opened to reveal angry venom dripping from his sharp fangs. Gage watched Viper's eyes squint down at the trembling cat below him.

"I'm going to give you one chance to run," Viper hissed. "If I ever see you disrespect my family again, I will swallow you whole."

Gage felt his tail release as Jesse jolted from the scene. Gage had never seen a cat run that fast. It wasn't until Gage glanced up again that he realized Viper was upset with him too.

"Why didn't you tell me what was happening?" Viper demanded.

"Because I didn't want your pity," Gage explained. "I was embarrassed. I thought I could handle it myself."

"But you shouldn't have to," Viper continued. "There's nothing to be embarrassed about. Jesse is a jerk. He singled you out, but it had nothing to do with you. I hope you understand that. It's obvious to everyone that Jesse feels like a joke. That's how he got *his* nickname. Jesse is fighting his own insecurities by bullying you. Bullies draw attention to others so that no one will notice where they fall short. I guarantee you that Jesse has a list of things he'd like to change about himself. I'd bet Jesse feels a lot smaller than you do.

"From now on, walk with self-worth, and rest assured that I have your back. All I ask is for you to check in from time to time. That's what families do."

Gage couldn't wait to catch his cold-blooded community up to speed.

31

ON POINT

Betsy sat with her team in the stairwell. She needed to give Gage an opportunity to reach the creek first. It was only natural that it would take Gage longer.

Betsy passed the time by listening as Mikey joked with Grey and Lane. Betsy guessed that Mikey's sudden chattiness was the result of nerves. Regardless, she couldn't help but laugh out loud at the longhair cat. She also found it hysterical that Mikey, Lane, and Grey had all decided to wear their costumes.

"Talk me through this," Mikey requested. "I mean, Grey, how did it start? One day you woke up and realized your words could move mountains? Turn flowers to fortune? Can you order my glasses to see life as rose-colored too?"

"It takes a lot more than glasses," Grey answered. "In a nutshell, I was born in a barn, grew up on a farm, and my mom, brother, and sister all live in the wild. I was raised by a Blue Jay, which everyone thinks is weird. I wouldn't be here without her."

"What's her name?" Mikey asked.

"Miss Jay," Grey said with a smile.

"Naturally," Mikey teased.

"A Black Widow Spider lived on the farm too," Grey continued. "The Widow had an ego that overshadowed other animals. We called it the Harrowing Hourglass. Eventually, the Widow and the ego were forced out of our barn. The Hourglass carried a lot of rage when they left, and it made a move for a hostile takeover on the farm. It even tried to force me to work for it as a double-agent spy. I had to forge my own path to survive.

"That's when I learned my voice had magic. I used it to shatter the hourglass of hate so that the Widow and I could both have a fresh start."

"Was it a straight-up ninja move?" Mikey wanted to know.

Grey laughed. "Dude, I've got moves you've never seen. Anyway, the experience taught me that there's always more to a story than meets the eye. In the Black Widow's case, she'd been forced to leave behind the only thing she knew. The Black Widow and I shared the same goal: We both wanted a home, wherever home was meant to be. We just needed to see that we weren't enemies after all."

"That's why I'm here, darlin'," Mikey insisted. "I've got the all-seeing glasses ready to roll. Next up, let's hear it for Lane with the magic ears. Tell us, when did you first become a fly on the wall?"

"Well, there aren't any spiders in my story," Lane began. "My mom was a show Lab. I've got two older brothers and two younger sisters. My brothers always teased me when we were young. One day, my left ear started zinging. Yes, like a fly was caught in it."

Lane and Mikey laughed.

"It drove me nuts," Lane continued. "I kept swatting at it. My brothers thought I was crazy. I started hearing voices and realized that one of them belonged to my sister. I was able to hear her thoughts. That's when I realized I could hear animals that I'm meant to assist."

Betsy noticed that Lane seemed lost in thought over his own answer. She wondered what Lane was thinking about.

Mikey turned to Scout. "What about you, Scout? Where are you from?"

Betsy felt the air shift as Scout turned to face her.

"Betsy, it's time," Scout stated. "Think you're ready for this?"

"I was born ready." Betsy smiled from ear to ear. "It's a walk in the park for dogs like us."

"You've got a seven-minute lead," Scout replied with a smirk. "Just pointing it out."

"Release the hounds," Betsy bantered, and winked.

. . . .

Betsy couldn't help herself. She felt the door shut behind her, and she took off and *ran*. She tore through the streets and didn't look back.

Betsy wasn't running to get ahead. She was running because she could. It was in her blood. The need for speed pulsed through her spotted dark blue body. Betsy wondered if the spots on her back, ears, and sides were scrambling to hold on. Scout had given her a seven-minute lead. Betsy chuckled at the very idea of being *given* a lead. In her experience, Betsy had always taken the lead.

Betsy knew Scout had been trained to zoom in on a target. Betsy understood that Scout didn't need her to sniff out an alternative plan. She sensed that Scout really just wanted her to sniff out any surprises. Betsy was betting on plenty of surprises today.

Betsy was half a mile down the Trinity Trails before she noticed that the trails were silent. The birds had stopped singing. Betsy guessed that the birds were hiding in their nests. The squirrels and raccoons appeared to be in lockdown too. Even the butterflies had disappeared.

Betsy assumed they were all analyzing her tail, which was on point. Usually that was a sign to the other animals to watch out. Betsy didn't have time to explain. The birds and the squirrels were safe. She wasn't running to chase anything down. The squirrels weren't even on her radar today.

Betsy followed her nose and continued with the plan. Her tongue wagged in the wind as she winked at the water cooler. She knew precisely where to go.

CHAPTER THIRTY-TWO

THE CROWD ROARED

G rey had hoped to use their time in the stairwell to think. About life. About herself. And about her team. Grey couldn't betray her Argos family, but she knew in her heart she couldn't hurt a stray cat either. It was like looking in the mirror and choosing a reflection. Who was she really facing? Barn or no barn, she had to honor every version of herself. Otherwise, her victory over the Harrowing Hourglass, and the quest for control over her identity, had been for nothing.

Grey had promised herself when she left BMF that she'd never forget her roots. She felt as much of a stray as she was a leash. The situation created a booming and unanswered question that crowded her mind and occupied her thoughts: Did the fork in the road represent failure or growth?

Only one way to find out, Grey thought to herself, as she followed her friends into the crowded unknown.

· · · · · · · ·

Grey had never stepped outside of the Argos. She'd never walked the city streets. Somehow, in the panic and the planning, she'd forgotten that small detail. Grey had always been with Blaze in a stroller. She suddenly realized that the skyline felt out of reach. The streetlights seemed blinding. For the first time in months, Grey felt small.

Grey walked alongside Scout. Grey noticed Scout's stride was purposeful. Not cocky like Lane's or smooth like Mikey's. With Scout, every step had a reason. Grey admired Scout's clarity. She hoped her words came as easily as his footing.

As the group approached the trail entrance, Grey saw Scout pause.

"I want you to stay as close to me as you can," Scout told her. "I'm not implying that you can't handle everything on your own; I know you can. I'll simply feel more comfortable if you and I stick together."

"No arguments here," Grey confirmed.

Grey crossed under the Trinity Trails gate. She felt life under her feet. She sensed history and heritage here, as though whatever lay underground was as vital as the air she breathed. The warm cement seemed to welcome her, as if Mr. Whistler himself was somehow waving below the long-forgotten tracks of his generosity. The skyscrapers, in all their glory, couldn't overlook the fact that they stood tall because the trails came first. The trails paved the way.

Grey felt the sunshine peek through the trees. It warmed her soul and coated her body with confidence. She studied the treetops too. They were so much different than her beloved pines. The Live Oaks were shorter and thicker with branches that spread out like the wings of angels.

Grey giggled as dandelion puffs flew by. They tickled her nose, her cheeks, but most of all her ears, which were ringing from the relentless chatter of the birds above. Cardinals and Blue Jays darted from tree to tree, while an eager Hummingbird zoomed by and landed on a nearby nest. Grey could hear the birds bantering back and forth. Grey knew birds were all gossip.

"Did you see the gecko this morning?" the Hummingbird asked once he caught his breath.

"I was told he walked the trails like he owned them."

"Doesn't he?" the Cardinal replied. "He earned that stride. He certainly went through enough. Look at that long tail now."

Grey sensed that the birds were talking about Gage. Grey wondered what Gage had been through. It had to have been something significant for these birds to follow his every move and talk about his return. Grey was deep in thought when she saw the sun spotlight a specific spot on the creek ahead. Grey reached for Scout's vest at the exact moment that Mikey called for their attention. The team was already working in unison.

"Hey, guys, I see something happening in these glasses," Mikey yelled. "It's only showing up in the glasses." Mikey flipped his black frames up and down on this face.

"The creek is covered in a sheet of leaves," Mikey continued. "The leaves are all holding on to one another like a raft. The leaves are carrying a black kitten from one side of the creek to the other. There are other black cats downstream, but they appear to have floated away. This black kitten is struggling and gasping for air. The leaves look like they're shouting at each other."

"The leaves were told to save that kitten," Lane reported. "Someone named Berma asked them to make sure the kitten made it across. They aren't happy about it, but it sounds like no one questions Berma. Berma saw the black kitten get separated from his family. She's watching and waiting for the kitten to make it across the creek."

"Scout, what do you think?" Grey asked.

Grey noticed that Scout seemed sad.

"Just that we need to know where the leaves dropped that kitten," Scout said, stiffening. "That's where we'll find Berma."

"Lead us!" Grey directed her magical voice. Grey watched her words roll into a ball and bounce down the trail. The foursome followed.

"The right words roll off the tongue," Grey said gently. "It's the wrong ones that get twisted."

"Twisted words travel too," Scout warned. "And often just as fast."

Grey heard the crowd's soft roar as the crooning birds looked on. Grey gathered that this was their first time witnessing the power of pure intention.

33

CHAPTER THIRTY-THREE
THE UNWILLING JUDGE

Berma knew this moment would come. She didn't know what it would look like, but she knew it would come. In a million years, she couldn't have anticipated a bouncing ball of words followed by a foursome of animals wearing costumes.

"Just when you thought you'd seen it all," Berma whispered to Oscar as the group approached.

"You must be Berma," Grey said with a smile. "My name is Grey. This is Scout, Lane, and Mikey."

"I am indeed," Berma replied. "And this is Oscar, the oldest Live Oak on the creek. So, tell me, to what do I owe this visit?"

"We'd like to learn about Davy," Scout replied. "Davy kidnapped animals from a nearby building. We're on a mission to rescue those animals. We're trying to understand why Davy would have done such a thing."

"Do you know Davy's story?" Grey asked.

"Better than anyone," Berma replied. "I've watched over Davy his whole life. Davy was born on the south side of the trails. He was separated from his family as a kitten. He survived and swam over to this very spot. He pulled himself out of the water, walked up the hill, and met Willow. Willow used to live in the white house. She was a widow in need of a companion. Davy stepped in and learned Willow's routines. He even learned her memories.

"Every day, Davy sat with Willow. Davy listened to Willow retell the same stories, over and over again. Davy was with Willow the night she died. He ran to the neighbor and yelled as loud as he could. When the ambulance arrived, Davy hid under my seat. We sat together the whole week. He was inconsolable.

"Davy watched as Willow's family mourned their loss. But it was Davy's loss too. As the last of Willow's friends left, Davy walked toward the front door. Davy had hoped to pay his respects to Willow's kids. Unfortunately, they weren't open to receiving it. The kids threatened Davy and chased him away. They even called him a stray. Davy had given his whole heart to Willow, and he had nowhere left to go.

"Oscar and I were devastated. We watched Davy jump straight back into the creek. Davy knew the water wasn't safe, but by that point, he'd decided that no place was safe. All we could do was hope that Davy would find shelter on the other side."

"That's when he started the Stray Club, isn't it?" Lane queried.

"Yes, it is," Berma confirmed.

"What can you tell us about the Stray Club?" Scout asked.

"It's very simple," Berma replied. "Animals help other animals in their time of need."

"How does Davy recruit new members?" Grey asked.

"Davy doesn't recruit anyone," Berma answered, smiling.

"Then how do animals discover the club?" Mikey asked.

"I think that depends on the animal," Berma acknowledged. "As I often say, we're not here to judge."

"How do *we* find the Stray Club?" Lane wanted to know.

"You may want to ask your friends," Berma said, pointing behind him.

Scout, Mikey, Lane, and Grey turned to find Betsy and Gage sitting in a metal boat by the water's edge.

Berma and Oscar watched the foursome race toward the boat.

"They still think this is just about Davy," Berma mused out loud.

Chapter Thirty-Four

The Captain and the Skipper

G age felt like a cross between a pirate and a prince. He could tell Betsy felt the same way . . . like royalty of some sort. Gage poked fun at his Bluetick buddy.

"A hero hidden as a hound," Gage said, and grinned.

"Riding alongside a captain chameleon," Betsy responded with a laugh.

Gage watched their crew approach. The foursome appeared desperate for answers and ready for a ride. Gage noticed that Scout seemed stoked to see the boat.

"This is a Patrol Trail boat," Gage offered. "It's the safest way to cruise the creek. These are the boats that officers use to patrol the trails at night. They call them PT Cruisers."

"How did we gain access to these cruisers?" Scout asked.

"Betsy sniffed out the opportunity," Gage replied. "She even nudged it over here with a little help from my family."

"Well, call me Skipper and hop on board!" Mikey shouted in a full sprint.

Gage watched Mikey run all the way to the bow of the boat before he remembered that they were surrounded by snakes. Hundreds of snake eyes stared back at the bright white cat. To Gage's delight, in the moment of truth, Mikey attempted a karate chop. Why Mikey went with that move was anyone's guess. To no one's surprise, Mikey missed the landing and rocked the boat, providing the snakes with a clear chance to lean in and share in the laugh. Mikey then raced down the center of the cruiser and cowered behind Scout. It took five minutes for the group to recover, including Mikey.

"Dude, nobody was moving," Gage said, rolling his eyes. "Or in danger. We've talked about this. The snakes are safe. A karate chop? Really? That was *your* move?"

"Laugh it up," Mikey muttered. "I've seen this dance before. Let's see if the longhair can swim. Next thing I know, the moccasins have me backed up against the boat while I'm begging for my mother. Go ahead and throw me to the sharks while you're at it."

"Shake it off, Skipper," Grey said, giggling.

"How about a shout out to the swimmers?" Lane suggested as he pointed to the snakes.

"Gage, perhaps an introduction, for good measure?" Scout added.

"Scout, Grey, Lane, Mikey . . . this is Viper," Gage said as he bowed to a senior snake.

Viper coiled his body, raised his head, and smiled to greet the group. Gage knew that smile all too well.

"Nice to meet you!" Viper said. "Any friend of Gage's is a friend of ours. You have the full support of our community today. We're going to push the boat because we don't want to crank the motor and draw attention to ourselves. I will personally guarantee your safety. I'll see to it that you make it across the creek and back."

"Thank you, Viper." Scout nodded in agreement.

Gage guessed that Viper and Scout probably had a lot in common. He realized they both bore the burden and pressure of protecting others.

"Is the strays' clubhouse directly across the creek?" Scout continued.

"It is," Viper confirmed. "Once we get halfway across, you'll see a large drainpipe by a set of stairs. The clubhouse was built under the stairs. They were both designed around the drainpipe, so the clubhouse completely blends in. It exists in harmony with the materials around it."

"Does the clubhouse back up to the water?" Scout inquired.

"Yes, and they used gravel for the flooring," Viper replied. "The rocky bottom creates a seamlessness with the water's edge. You can't tell where the water stops and the house starts. You'll see what I mean as we get closer. The only marker is a sign on the porch with the letters *SOS* written on it."

"Are you saying the Stray Club literally wrote 'SOS'?" Scout asked.

"Davy wrote it," Viper verified.

"It's your call," Gage spoke directly to Scout. "How do you want us to approach?"

"Carefully," Scout calculated. "We're going to need everyone involved. I'd like for the snakes to swarm the house and hang upside down from the roof. Not to attack anyone. Just get in a position to dive into the house if—and only if—it's absolutely necessary.

"Gage, we'll need you to stay on the shore and hold on to the boat. You can stick to the outside and anchor it in place until you find another way to secure it. We'll use Lane's ears, Mikey's eyes, and Grey's voice to get into position. We can charge the room together. I'll go in first, followed by Grey, Lane, Betsy, and Mikey.

"There's no way to know what we're walking into. SOS is a distress signal, so we should be mindful of that. All of these animals have stories. We don't know how they ended up at the Stray Club. I have a strange feeling that we'll be searching for more than just the board today. I don't know why. We need to see the full picture."

"This is your mission," Gage acknowledged. "I'll hold down the fort."

"And I'll follow your lead," Betsy seconded.

"Aye, aye, Captain!" Gage added.

35

CHAPTER THIRTY-FIVE
House Rules

D avy thought back to those early memories sitting on the porch. Days felt like weeks. Time stood still. The sweltering heat stayed well past sunset, and Davy joked that Rand had the unfair advantage of a built-in shade. Had it not been for the sunset, neither Davy nor Rand would have known when day became dusk. On cue, the Creek Quartet erupted in rapture. The musical notes carried themselves like sweet tea to a parched glass. The notes offered relief. They were refreshing and kind to the soul. Davy and Rand drank in music to the last drop. Davy watched the porch become a melody of summertime bliss.

Rand spent most of his afternoons swimming along the lazy river of their shoreline. Davy watched his friend pretend to float by on his shell. Davy laughed as the turtle waved with his feet in the air. The water wrapped around Rand like a friend in a cool embrace.

Over time, Davy found forgotten scraps that could be used for furniture. He scored when a family left behind an entire picnic basket. Piece by piece, Davy carried each item to the clubhouse. He picked up two glasses, two plates, two dinner napkins, and a blanket. The napkins were brown and monogrammed with delicate pink flowers. Davy used them as window coverings to block the balmy heat. The matching brown blanket offered cushioning for the floor, but the final touch came as jasmine blossomed through the wood-laden walls. Foliage and white flowers filled the room with fragrant ambition. Davy wondered if Willow's garden hadn't relocated for the purpose of looking after him.

Other animals trickled in slowly. The animals came from all over the country. Each had their reasons.

Davy and Rand took the time to hear every tale. It had been Rand that realized they needed to establish a few guidelines for the guests. Rand didn't want to risk word spreading about their house to anyone that wouldn't respect Camp David.

"Can I get everyone's attention?" Davy shouted over the noise of the crowd. "I'm thrilled that you're here. I welcome you. I'm looking forward to learning more about what you need. Before we jump into that, I'd like to share a few house rules.

"The first rule at Camp David is that I want you to talk about Camp David. Let's call it the Stray Club. Share it. Share your story. Share it among the animals that need to feel inspired. Just be careful of what you say and whom you say it to. We need to work together to keep this a safe space. We have an open-door policy. We do not discriminate against dogs, cats, frogs, fish, birds, or snakes.

"The second rule at Camp David and the Stray Club is that you must take pride in being a stray. Own who you are. I promise, you do you better than anyone else. So many animals are at war with themselves. They listen to the chatter and begin to feel less than enough. Maybe they're comparing themselves to other animals. You shouldn't follow that herd. I hope you rediscover your sense of self at Camp David. Find that 'thing' that makes you *you*. Then wave it around like a flag. Let's line up our flags and watch them wave together. I'll bet they blow by the winds of change.

"The third and final rule of Camp David and the Stray Club is that you must commit to seeing and hearing other animals. That sounds obvious, but it isn't. Look all animals in the eye. Life's too short to look the other way. Listen for where you're needed. A life without service is no life at all. Think of yourselves as the gatekeepers of ground zero. This is a fresh start for many animals in search of their best self. Honor that, and you'll pay your visit at Camp David forward."

The crowd cheered as Davy sat down beside Rand. Davy saw the very red-eared turtle smile.

"How'd I do?" Davy whispered.

"You did great," Rand replied. "How does it feel?"

"Like I just emptied my suitcase," Davy declared.

"Then you can finally fly," Rand replied. "And so can they."

Own who

you are.

36

CHAPTER THIRTY-SIX

THE FINAL COUNTDOWN

Grey looked from the boat to the sea of snakes swimming around her. Everyone had a reason for being there. Even the snakes made sense. Everything seemed in order, but something didn't feel right. It felt *too* orderly. They'd arrived on a boat, en route to a secret space while surrounded by snakes. Was her team that good? Perhaps. They'd all brought special skills to the table. They'd all been called upon for their extraordinary gifts. Grey couldn't place the uneasiness in her gut. She felt as if the answer was staring straight at her. She just didn't know where to look.

Grey remembered each of George's notes. Not one piece of information had been specifically directed at Mikey, Lane, or herself. Yet George knew he was leaving the three of them with the task of solving this very strange puzzle. George had led them to Crown, and Crown clearly and without hesitation led them to Scout. Their entire mission had been choreographed and developed by Scout. What did they really know about him? Grey hunkered down in the boat as her board's safety hung in the balance.

"What's wrong?" Lane asked.

"Something," Grey replied.

· · · · · · · ·

Grey studied the house ahead. Viper's description had been spot-on. The mossy wood made the home unnoticeable to passersby.

Grey felt the boat slow down. The snakes stopped short of the shore, just as Scout had requested. Grey watched Scout motion to each of their teammates. At her turn, Grey verbally confirmed that she was ready. Grey saw Scout give the go-ahead to Viper. The mission was "A Go." Grey knew the rest of the plan would move fast.

Viper led the boat ashore. The Trinity Trails snakes slithered up to the clubhouse. The moccasins moved with lightning speed, racing over the rocks like warriors. Grey watched the snakes cover the roof just as Scout had directed.

Grey's eyes glanced at Lane, who had dashed to the front door. As instructed, Lane appeared to be listening for any hidden threats. Grey watched Mikey walk stealthily behind Lane, one paw at a time, squinting as his eyes sought any sign of movement.

"See anything?" Scout asked.

"The room is filled with animals, and they might be tied up," Mike whispered. "It looks that way with or without the glasses. Who knows? You OK?"

"My heart's beating out of my chest," Scout whispered. "I can't remember the last time I felt this alive."

"Me too," Grey admitted.

Grey followed Scout as they slid into position. Grey listened as Scout counted down from 3, 2, 1. She watched for her cue to say the magic words. . . .

"Open the door," Grey ordered.

Grey watched her words remove the only remaining barrier to their Argos board members. She then followed Scout in the official charge against the Stray Club.

Grey thought her team was ready for anything on the other side of that door. She was wrong. Team 6 burst into the clubhouse. Shortly thereafter, they burst into tears.

37

Chapter Thirty-Seven
Cloud Nine

Polly listened to the beating hearts below. It was music to her ears.

"He felt it," Ali declared.

"No doubt," Polly responded. "They all did. How do you feel?"

"Giddy," Ali said with a grin.

"Are we all ready for what's next?" Polly rallied the crew.

"Are you kidding me?" Mi beamed. "Who doesn't love a big reveal?"

Polly, Gamma, Beta, Merak, Dubhe, Co, and Ali laughed. As planned, they were floating together on Cloud Nine.

"We're going that way," Dubhe said, pointing.

"Giddyup," Polly replied.

"Follow me," Dubhe directed.

Polly twinkled and jumped behind Ali, eager to see the stars take a much-deserved victory lap.

38

CHAPTER THIRTY-EIGHT

THE SILENT SALUTE

G rey felt the air shift as she entered the Stray
Club. Grey immediately noticed that the room
was completely full. Animals of all types stood
shoulder to shoulder, lined up in even rows. Their hands
and paws were raised in the air. They each appeared to
be holding a flag of some sort. To Grey's dismay, the
animals also appeared to be tied together. The Argos

board members were positioned front and center, as if on display. Grey saw that the board members were still in their costumes too.

Grey's back legs moved in position to charge.

"Wait!" Scout shouted.

Grey paused for a split second. In that second, everything changed.

Grey gasped as each animal's flag floated and rose in the room. Grey watched the snakes outside the windows yank an interconnected string. The snakes weren't hanging upside down, as planned. Instead, they were posted like flagpoles, angled away from the clubhouse, with a string wrapped around their cold-blooded and coiled bodies.

"Look at the snakes!" Grey screamed.

"Look at the flags!" Scout insisted.

Grey realized that there were flags in every color of the rainbow. Some were striped, while others had wavy marks resembling fish scales. They were all different, clearly representing the varying animals in the room. A yellow flag featured a drawing of a fish with a lightning bolt. A purple flag had a cardinal sitting on a music chord. Grey saw pride in the self-portraits. She then noticed what looked to be the official flag of the Stray Club. Paw prints were stamped in paint around a circular black crest. Grey read "The Stray Club" written along the arch at the bottom of the crest, and "Camp David" written along the arch at the top.

Grey suddenly realized that the animals had repositioned themselves. Some were now standing with their right forelegs bent and their paws pointed at their temples. They seemed united, and safe, in their new silent salute.

Grey turned around to find a red, white, and blue flag mounted to the wall in front of the animals. Grey remembered Scout's vest and patch. She saw that her teammate was sobbing. Her entire team was crying uncontrollably.

"This is about you," Grey whispered to Scout. Grey knew they had all reached the same conclusion. "The Stray Club is honoring you."

Grey had just processed the flags when a group of stars burst through the brown curtains. Team 6 ducked as the stars darted to position, spelling the word *Twin* in the air. They spread out from wall to wall as they caught their breath, as if they had been racing to get to this very room at this very moment.

Grey had a feeling that while the flags flew for the group, the stars had arrived for one animal in particular. Based on Scout's expression, Grey guessed the word *Twin* made a lot more sense to him.

Grey had expected a battle. She'd been prepared to fight. She was suddenly unsure who was fighting whom, or whether any battle lines had been drawn at all. She was surrounded by flags, stars, and an assortment of animals, all of whom continued to know way more about Team 6 than Team 6 knew about them. Grey was reminded of the question she had asked herself on her first night in the city: "Who really pushes the buttons around here?"

39

CHAPTER THIRTY-NINE
OSS

D avy took one look at Scout and knew the Stray Club existed for animals like him.

Davy introduced himself. "Hi, Scout, my name is Davy. It is our great honor to have you here today. We want to start by thanking you for your work and ongoing service on the front lines."

"Grey, Mikey, and Lane, we are safe," George added.

"What's going on?" Grey demanded.

"What does *Twin* mean?" Lane barked.

"What are the stars doing here?" Mikey asked.

"What'd I miss?" Gage blurted out as he barged into the room behind his team.

"Davy and George were just about to explain why no one appears to be in danger," Lane said, seething.

"Why don't you all take a seat?" George suggested. "Let us explain."

Davy knew this was going to be an emotional day for Scout. Davy could also tell that Grey, Lane, and Mikey had lost their patience in the process. They looked utterly confused and very irritated. Davy waited for their new guests to gather themselves and take a seat. He watched the stars regroup in the corner to chat.

"Perhaps I can start," Davy began. "By now, I'm sure you've heard a lot about me. I'd like to fill in the gaps. Then we can share how it came to be that our stories all overlap."

Davy paused to glance over at the Argos board members. They all nodded their heads in agreement.

"I help other animals," Davy continued. "I'm a good listener because I've been both a house cat and a stray. I've spent as much time on a comfy couch as I have on the creek. I built this place to redefine what the word *stray* meant. To me, *stray* means 'self.' To be stray means you're independent. You're a survivor. You're a leader. You're strong, and you have the courage to step up, no matter what anyone else says.

"Every stray has taken the time to learn about themselves. Some had to reach the clubhouse before they could do it. Others just needed a minute to share their story and feel seen. In feeling seen, they rediscovered who they really were to begin with.

"Here's what I can tell you for sure: Members of the Stray Club will always look you in the eye. We find it funny that the animals on leashes won't look back. It's just a matter of perspective. We take pride in who we've become. We applaud one another and celebrate one another's accomplishments."

"Who actually lives here?" Grey asked.

"Rand and I do," Davy answered. "Rand arrived shortly after I finished building the place. It took him a long time to get here. We immediately knew that we'd make a good team. We then saw an opportunity to help other animals move forward and take flight on their journey."

Davy paused to smile at Rand.

"Animals come and go," Rand continued. "The hope is that they come to share, and they leave to give back. Animals always leave something behind."

Rand pointed to a table in the back of the room. It was filled with gifts left behind by members of the Stray Club.

"How did you meet the animals from the Argos?" Lane inquired.

"I can step in here," Blaze began. "As you know, my story's a bit different."

Blaze paused to let her friends enjoy a well-deserved laugh.

"I had a human before I had a heartbeat. How privileged is that? My original mom, Jules, handed me off to her son, Stan. It wasn't tragic. I wasn't homeless. I was humbled and discarded. The experience made me scared that I wasn't good enough anymore. I lost faith in myself. When Anne appeared with Grey, I worried that Grey would replace me. To be honest, I didn't even recognize myself."

"I thought you thought I wasn't good enough," Grey mustered up the courage to say.

"You're the best barn burner in town," Blaze bantered.

Grey blushed.

"It took me a while to feel that way," Blaze said, grinning. "I roamed the building at night trying to think of a way to get rid of you. It was going to be a 'Blaze of Glory' kind of moment."

Grey nodded in Lane's direction and grinned.

"Instead, I came across Scout," Blaze continued. "He was sitting in the stairwell. I didn't know anything about him. I saw his tattered vest and tired body. I stopped in my tracks. It immediately reminded me that I'd lived a very charmed life, safe from disaster. I know it's all relative, but that one moment watching Scout in the stairwell put everything else in perspective."

"I never saw you," Scout stated.

"I know," Blaze confirmed. "I quietly crept back up the stairs. The next day I spoke to George. We knew from your vest that you were an official service dog, which meant you'd been trained to put other animals' needs above your own. We could also tell you needed help. George mapped out a kidnapping coup. Our hope was that it would remind you of your value. I felt like finding you had restored my faith. Seeing you shook sense back into me. You helped me understand how lucky my situation actually was. It was my intention to restore *your* faith too. I wasn't sure if you needed help restoring faith in yourself or faith in your future. Perhaps both. Either way, I wanted to step up. George and I decided to call the mission 'Operation Search and Save: OSS.'

"We had a secret meeting with Crown, Olivia, and Meg. Unlike the other leashes, I had heard great things about Camp David and the Stray Club. I knew the club focused on this sort of thing. I also knew that Davy was very careful about honoring the intention of the club. I suggested a marketing brochure to advertise the Argos . . . but it was really just an easy way to drop a message to Davy with information about our mission. Olivia planned the whole mixer around the board members' disappearance."

"I knew I could trust the team from Unleashed Events," Olivia offered. "If anyone began to suspect us, Connie would have an answer for it. I also knew that Gage's connections to the creek moccasins would hold up. Plus, we all had a hunch that Scout would respect Betsy's training. So, I snuck Davy, Connie, Betsy, and Gage into the maintenance closet. We waited until the time was right to set up for the party."

"And Crown?" Lane asked. "What was his role? I know he had one."

"Everyone trusts Crown," George agreed. "Crown honors all of our individual gifts. He guards our privacy. We knew Crown could connect with you, and he'd know which card to play. Crown was your guide."

"Crown also knew that I had misjudged the Stray Club," Lane acknowledged. "I now realize I was one of the leashes that had this all wrong."

Davy caught the shared glance between Grey and Lane. He sensed this day would forever bond the two friends.

"You had to work as a team today," Davy spoke. "You had to see things through someone else's eyes and speak up on their behalf. You were forced to listen to someone else's story and learn how that story impacted their path. You did this while staying true to your own personal power and never losing sight of the individual strengths you brought to the table. There is no truer example of teamwork. There is no clearer sign of character. You all put someone else's needs above your own in search of an answer."

"Speaking of that, Scout, do you want to share your story?" Grey asked. "How did you end up in the stairwell at the Argos? And how did the stars get involved?"

Davy watched Scout shift in his vest. Davy's eyes raced over to Rand. Davy and Rand both knew it would take work to shed the weight of pressure Scout had placed on himself. They also knew it would take time to unpack Scout's past.

"Take all the time you need," Rand encouraged.

40

CHAPTER FORTY

STATION CHIEF

S cout scanned the room. He'd never shared his story, but somehow, he felt strangely safe to do so here. He'd just met many of these animals. He saw them as he saw himself.

"My nickname is 'Twin,'" the Golden Retriever began. "I come from a long lineage of dogs trained to search and rescue under the most extreme circumstances. I'm part of a national urban search and rescue team and a member of Task Force 1. My team is called in to help when bad things happen, like hurricanes, fires, and national disasters. We are the canine first responders, always on the front line. My grandmother was part of the same task force team. In fact, she was its most famous member. Because of her, this vest is all I've ever known.

"I've always followed in my grandmother's footsteps. She taught me everything I know. She was one of the canine heroes of 9/11. When airplanes hit the Twin Towers on September 11th in New York City, task forces around the country stepped up to assist in the search for survivors. My grandmother's team arrived in New York the very next day. She made friends with the animals from coast to coast that were stationed alongside her. That's where she first saw the stars. They lit the sky from one side to the other. Night after night, the stars guided her.

"To honor my grandmother's service, the stars promised to light her path from that point forward.

"I've always known that the stars played a role in my grandmother's life, but I didn't realize until now that they would appear for me too."

Scout paused to smile and offer an expression of his gratitude.

"How's that for an intro?" Polly said, beaming. "I'm Polly, the North Star. Scout's grandmother was a dear friend. She asked that I never let Scout out of my sight. That was her dying wish. So I assembled a team of rock stars to help guide Scout on his journey in life. We try to put some day-to-day distance between us, but we've always kept our promise."

"Following my grandmother's success at ground zero, she went on to work at sites impacted by Hurricanes Rita and Katrina," Scout continued. "She was a hero in every way."

"Those are big shoes to fill," Grey commented.

"And big shoes cast a big shadow," Scout stated sadly.

"When I built Camp David, I told myself I was laying the foundation for something big," Davy shared. "I literally said I was starting fresh from ground zero. I even thought about that when I established the house rules for the Stray Club. The metaphor behind our membership is that we're all starting from ground zero. Your stars led you here today so that we can honor *you*, just as you honor your grandmother every day."

Scout watched the animals and stars nod in agreement. He felt overwhelmed by their grace and empathy.

"I arrived at the Argos because I was on my own mission," Scout recounted. "All search and rescue dogs have trainers. My grandmother had the same trainer, or partner, her whole life. She was a firefighter. My partner was too. His name is Graham. We worked as a team for years. We traveled wherever we were needed. Contrary to what you think, Blaze isn't the most ferocious cat I've come across." Scout paused to smile at Blaze.

"Graham understood that I struggled to live up to the expectations of who I was supposed to become. My friends called me 'Twin' because of my grandmother's service at the Twin Towers. Graham was different, though. He pushed me to find my own path. Graham called me the 'Eagle.' It was his special name for me. He said that no dog had ever been born with eagle eyes or reflexes as sharp as mine. He encouraged me to stand tall.

"A few months ago, Graham got called to serve in California. They needed expert firefighters. I was told to remain at my station because my team needed me. I watched Graham leave. It was the worst day of my life.

"I was reassigned to a new person, but to be honest, my heart wasn't in it. We didn't have the same connection. I struggled and worried that I had somehow failed. Failed the task force. Failed my grandmother. Maybe I'd somehow even failed myself. I still want to serve, but I need to do so with Graham. So, I decided to leave on a mission to find him. I didn't ask for permission. They have a word for that . . . it's called going AWOL."

"What's AWOL?" a young cat asked.

"It means that I left without notice," Scout replied. "It means that some will say I've gone missing. I probably can't go back. Leaving as I did is considered dishonorable."

Scout closed his eyes, as though hiding from his self-induced shame.

"But aren't we all AWOL in some way?" the young cat continued.

"What do you mean?" Scout quietly inquired.

"Animals WithOut Leashes," the young cat offered.

"Indeed, and there's an honor code here too," Davy declared.

"What's your code?" Scout questioned.

"We serve from the core of our best selves," Davy divulged.

"What makes that a team effort?" Scout scoffed.

"We remind you that you are enough," Davy proclaimed.

"When you shine, we all shine, and our flags wave as one," Rand revealed.

"I bet your grandmother had a very strong sense of who she was," Davy declared.

"She never questioned herself," Scout agreed. "It defined her as a leader."

"It always does," Davy affirmed.

"Scout, what's your plan?" Grey inquired. "Where do you go from here?"

"I'm headed west to California," Scout relayed. "That's been the plan all along. I just got tired and needed to rest. I saw a blond dog outside of the Argos and followed her into the building."

Scout bared a sheepish grin.

"I understand," Lane said with a laugh. "I've lost days following that same dog."

The room erupted in much-needed hysteria.

"I figured it had to be a safe spot, so I caught the Argos back door before it closed," Scout continued. "I noticed that the lights were out in the stairwell. I knew I could hide there until I built my strength back up.

"That's when Grey, Lane, Crown, and Mikey found me. I listened to their story. I knew instantly that I could help, so I stepped up. To be honest, it felt good. It reminded me of my purpose. By serving them, I regained the confidence that I need to continue. I suppose I found a new station, too."

"Your station is your soul," Grey said. "It goes where you go. Take my word for it. I left a lot behind to get here too. Your 'special force' resides chiefly within you.

Integrity makes you a hero. That vest didn't lead you to the Argos or to Camp David. Your moral compass did. I bet Polly would call that true north."

Scout saw Polly wink from above.

"That's how we all ended up here today," Rand recapped. "We sit among heroes from all walks of life and light."

"I have an idea," Grey said. She stood and stared at George, Blaze, Olivia, and Meg. "We need to help Scout find Graham. We completed your OSS mission. Now we should find a way to help Scout on his mission to make it out west. We need a new plan."

"Here, here!" Lane cheered. "Let's hear it for the wild, wild West!"

Scout watched Grey shimmy in her western dress as she moved over to hug him.

"You do realize this vest is for real, right?" Scout said, smiling at his new friend.

. . . .

Scout sat in silence and smiled at the stars. They remained in the corner of the room, teasing Polly as she reenacted a tale. Scout knew the stars were there to continue guiding his journey. He also recognized that every animal in the room would join forces to help him on the most important search of his life.

Is this a search for myself, or my partner? Scout pondered.

Scout realized that the two roads had intersected. He unfastened his vest and pulled open the zipper on the inside left pocket. He removed the blue handkerchief that Graham had left behind. Graham had always worn the handkerchief on important missions. Graham called it his "Chief." Scout smiled as he remembered the mantra Graham repeated every time that he tied the handkerchief around his neck: "To become a chief, you must champion for all."

Scout held the handkerchief in his paw before raising it to his nose, and then his heart. In that moment, Scout felt a shudder, as though somewhere in the distance, far, far ahead, Graham was championing for him.

"I'm coming," Scout promised, both to himself and his human.

*To become
a chief, you
must champion
for all.*

41

THE GIVING TABLE

Mikey listened to the flags flap. Even as the wind whipped, the totems of teamwork stood tall.

Mikey had stepped outside to take a moment to reflect on life before the Argos. He had been born on the streets. Not the trails—the streets. Mikey was born in a box behind an old building. He was an alley cat, at least ten notches below the trails. His mom and dad raided the restaurant trash for food every night. However, in Mikey's mind, they ate like kings.

Mikey didn't know that his family was poor until other animals told him. He questioned what it meant to be poor. He may have eaten discarded food, but there was nothing trashy about him. Mikey was an elegant cat. He had a style of his own from the very start.

Mikey learned pretty quicky that he'd have to fend for himself. So he did. Mikey's mornings were spent with his mom. Together they made sure their box stayed safe. The city also kept a close watch on their street to make sure that businesses kept things clean. Crews came by every morning, which gave Mikey the afternoons to explore the surrounding neighborhoods.

Mikey started by watching the street kids dance. They sat around in a circle and took turns playing songs. Mikey learned rhythm and beats from those kids. He got his swagger from the street.

Mikey then moved from the music scene to the sidewalk shops. He scoured every shop within a ten-block radius. He imagined the day when he'd have a house all to himself and fill it with his favorite items from the shops. Rain or shine, Mikey always stopped by The Head Hut. It was his turnaround point—the ten-block marker. The entire shop was dedicated to things worn from the neck up. Scarves. Jewelry. Sunglasses. They were all organized by color. Mikey loved the black sunglasses the best. There was a pair in particular that framed his face perfectly.

One rainy day, Mikey had been shocked to see those glasses in the trash outside the shop. He noticed that they were scratched. That must have been the reason the glasses were discarded. Mikey didn't care about the scratch. He grabbed the glasses and ran.

Mikey made it around the block before he put the sunglasses on. He stood in the rain wearing the only thing he'd ever owned. The world walked around him. Mikey didn't realize that other alley cats had been watching him. The animals lunged at Mikey, but a passerby stepped in to break up the brawl. Mikey watched the cats pick up his displaced glasses. They snickered as they scurried away. But in a serendipitous twist of fate, the passerby picked up Mikey and took him home.

That day, the worst day, Mikey lost his only possession. That same day, Mikey gained his very own home. Home to the human who healed him. Home to the dumpster that gifted him a new set of glasses. Home to the friends that offered unconditional love. The Argos animals never asked Mikey why he wore those glasses all the time.

Mikey glanced through the window. The strays reminded him of his days as an alley cat. The days when class and character inhabited the same beaten box. The strays didn't need a leash to feel loved. Like Mikey, they didn't even know they were poor.

Mikey entered the clubhouse and passed a group of animals gathered on the rug. He walked straight to the "Giving Table" in the back of the room. From flowers to feathers, the table was covered with items left behind as a token of gratitude.

"You OK back here?" Grey approached.

Mikey smiled as he removed his black glasses.

"These glasses have served me well," Mikey mused. "I think with the right owner, they could become rose-colored after all. I bet a stray could see their unlimited potential. That's my hope for whoever finds them next. My glasses are my gift. They've come full circle."

Mikey placed his glasses on the table, grateful for the reminder of just how far he'd come. He then watched Grey reach for the blue stone she'd been carrying under the belt of her costume. Grey set the stone on the table beside Mikey's glasses.

"I think this stone was on a journey to get here too," Grey said. "Perhaps it will help someone share their story or discover their voice. That's my hope for whoever finds it next."

Mikey watched the table welcome the new additions.

Together, Mikey and Grey read the mantra posted on the plank above the table:

CAMP DAVID:

The visiting hours,
Of a temporary stay.
We packed our bags,
We wore our tags,
And here we are today.

So, stand here beside us,
A friend among the strays.
We'll hear you,
And see you,
Long after parting ways.

42

THE DOCK

Grey sensed that it was time. The sun warned that the end of the day was drawing near.

"Betsy, you're going to get us safely across the creek, right?" Grey inquired.

"You bet," Betsy confirmed. "The snakes are ready, and Davy is going to ride with us. We'll hop out where you guys jumped in earlier. Then Davy will bring the boat back over here. Davy can hold on to the boat for as long as he needs it—or as long as he can get away with it. But we're going to have to run to make it home in time."

"Blaze and I will jump on Lane's bathmat," Grey said with a grin.

"Watch out for the trailblazers!" Blaze grinned back.

"I'm going to give Gage and Meg a lift," George confirmed.

"That might be a hard no for me," Gage countered. "I'll see how the sea legs hold up."

"Well, I'm going to beat *everyone* to the Argos," Olivia announced.

"And Scout?" Grey asked. "You're sure about this? You want to rest up with Rand?"

"Rand has walked this country from coast to coast," Scout stated. "We're going to map out my path. The stars have suggestions too. We'll be in touch soon."

"We'll send word with Gage when it's time to regroup and decide who's going with Scout," Rand replied.

"I'll be back and forth between the Argos and the creek," Gage said, nodding. "I've got that part covered."

"OK, let's do this," Davy said. He smiled and gathered the group for a final hug.

Grey took one last look around the room. She noted the exact placement of the Giving Table, the embroidered window coverings, and even the worn-out rug. Grey memorized the room. She wanted to see it when she closed her eyes. Grey would always see the Stray Club.

"Come on!" the others yelled. Grey ran from the front door, across the gravel, and onto the boat. Grey sat beside Davy as the snakes pushed the boat quickly across the creek. Grey noticed that Davy had grown quiet as they passed the halfway mark. Grey followed Davy's eyes, which seemed to be staring at the shoreline.

"What's wrong?" Grey asked. Grey could tell by Davy's facial expression that he was growing more serious by the minute.

"Where exactly did you guys jump into the boat before?" Davy asked.

Grey retraced the afternoon. It had all gone by in a blur.

"Betsy and Gage had the boat sitting on the dock at the . . ." Grey stopped.

"Where?" Davy demanded.

"Sitting on the dock at the white house, behind Berma the Bench," Grey admitted.

Grey suddenly wondered if there had been two Stray Club missions: one for Scout, and one for Davy.

Was that possible? If so, which of her teammates had arranged for this to happen? Grey realized they were about to pull up on the dock behind Davy's old house. Grey could tell that Davy was uncomfortable. Maybe even angry. Definitely confused.

CHAPTER FORTY-THREE

A STONE'S THROW

S cout watched the snakes swarm as his team floated over the horizon. He knew he would see them again.

"He has no idea," Rand shared.

"What an uphill battle," Scout concluded.

"Yes, but now he's ready," Rand confirmed.

"Two houses, a stone's throw apart," Scout marveled.

"He needed to build his foundation," Rand answered.

"That's a lot of work to end up right back where you started," Scout stated.

"Some animals have to see life on the other side to know how good they have it," Rand replied. "Others, like Davy, just need a minute to rediscover their potential. Often it's as simple as seeing a sign and having faith that you're on the right track."

Scout saw Rand's eyes move from the SOS letters to the stars resting on the clubhouse roof.

"Words of wisdom from a traveled turtle," Scout surmised.

44

CHAPTER FORTY-FOUR

THE NATURE OF NOW

Polly saw the sun move across the sky. As the golden hour light emerged, so too would shadows in the distance. Polly's eyes flickered from the sun to the stars with a watchful gaze. Polly was always on high alert as to what could be hiding in the shadows.

"We made it this far," Merak said, sighing with relief.

"We're exactly where we said we'd be," Polly confirmed.

"It revolves around her from here." Dubhe pointed to the sun.

"Tomorrow's a new day," Polly agreed. "The sun will guide us, but we have a long road ahead. These animals have a lot of ground to cover."

"Hence the reason to find joy right here, right now," Ali affirmed.

"Isn't it something?" Beta observed. "Mother Earth has a totally different perspective."

"It's the climate," Gamma agreed. "It's changing here."

"We have a lot of work to do," Polly asserted as she settled in to watch the sunset from the metal roof of Camp David. She'd heard the view from the Stray Club was spectacular. Polly glowed with gratitude as the skyline shifted from pale blue to neon orange to electric pink. The orchestra of crickets and creek animals ensued, marking the moment with a chorus of universal connection.

CHAPTER FORTY-FIVE

THE HOMECOMING

Betsy was the first to jump out of the boat.
Betsy knew Davy was going to have a lot
of questions, but she needed to send the Argos
group away first. Betsy laughed as Lane adjusted his
brown bathmat, giving Blaze just enough rope to bolt
it down on his back and make handles to hold on.

"Grey, I'll jump on first and get settled," Blaze
offered. "You're smaller. You can hop in front of me."

255

Betsy stepped up to offer support as the two cats carefully slipped into their spots.

"The Trail Ranger and the Rhinestone Sheriff," Betsy barked.

Grey grabbed the handles and leaned into Lane's neck.

"We're knee-deep in it now, aren't we?" Grey joked.

"Deep in what is the question," Lane quipped.

"Deep in the land of the strays," Blaze answered, beaming.

Betsy giggled as George bent down on the grass. He got low enough for Meg and Gage to jump on his back. The whole scene was straight out of a comedy skit. Meg moved around and scooted back onto George's back as Gage squeezed in front of her, all while waving his arms like a lasso in Lane's direction.

"Betsy, are you coming?" Lane asked.

"Nope, I'm going to stay with Davy," Betsy replied.

"Sounds good," Lane said. "Davy, we'll see you soon!"

Betsy watched her teammates race off toward the Argos. She turned to Davy and took a deep breath. Betsy knew it was now or never.

"Davy, I think it's time for you to come home," Betsy began.

"What are you talking about?" Davy said, confused.

"I live here now, in your old house," Betsy continued. "The white house on the hill. Willow's kids sold the house to my humans. We moved in shortly after Willow passed away. The kids told us all about David and Willow. They watched the trails become what they are today.

"After we moved in, I started making friends on the creek. I met Gage by the water cooler, and we decided to work together. You and I both know that everything happens for a reason. We met with Olivia and learned about the Argos mission to help Scout. We knew they were planning to work with the Stray Club. I saw it as fate. I decided to use the opportunity—the mission—to also bring you back here, to your house. I wanted to give you the chance to stay this time, on your terms.

"I talked to Berma about my plan. We came up with the idea to dock the boat here. That way Lane, Mikey, and Grey wouldn't think twice about returning to this spot. Obviously, Gage knows where I live. The others don't.

"My family wants a cat. They've been waiting for the right one. They call me Queen Betsy. If I'm on board, they're on board. Come with me, and I promise you'll be welcomed into our family on the spot."

257

"I have obligations," Davy replied. "It's not that simple now. I can't just leave Rand and the clubhouse behind. I started something. I can't go back on my word. You don't get to leave your commitments behind just because something better comes along."

"You're not leaving," Betsy replied. "You laid the foundation. The Stray Club is part of you, and it's just across the creek. You can visit anytime. Camp David exists to lift animals up, not hold them down. By following your path, you've already created the house rules that work for you. You built the structure before you even knew you would need it. You just knew that it needed to be built. Because of you, the Stray Club will bring that same faith to lots of other animals.

"Rand and I have already talked about it. Rand is staying at the Stray Club. He's your wingman, after all. He spent his whole life en route to the clubhouse. The clubhouse is *his* permanent home. The point is that it doesn't have to be yours."

"You're sure Rand is OK with this?" Davy whispered.

"He knows this is what's best for both of you," Betsy confirmed. "So, are you ready to come home?"

Betsy paused as Davy looked from the creek to Oscar, from Oscar to Berma, and from Berma to the white house at the top of the hill. Betsy sensed that Davy was taking a second to honor his past, just as Mr. Whistler would have wanted.

"The trees along the front of the house are new," Davy noticed.

"They're called Desert Willow trees," Betsy replied. "Jojo planted them in honor of Willow. Jojo's probably at the house now, wearing her overalls."

"Does the sunroom still smell like pound cake?" Davy asked as he wiped away a tear. "Actually, don't answer that. Let's go meet your family."

"Our family, brother." Betsy smiled. "This is our house now."

CHAPTER FORTY-SIX

THE COLORS OF CHANGE

G rey wrapped the reins around her arms and leaned into Lane's back. Her legs had begun to throb. She shut her eyes, held her breath, and listened as Blaze whispered the play-by-play in her perked ear.

"We're almost there," Blaze offered. "Hold on! Whatever you do, don't let go!"

Grey was grateful to be sandwiched between her two roommates. She was even more grateful to pull up at the back of the Argos building.

Grey released the rope and hugged the sidewalk the second they arrived. As planned, they watched Gage race for the front entrance. He was the only one small enough to sneak through the front door without being seen. Gage had to get to Connie so she could let them in through the back door.

"All we can do is wait," Grey concluded.

"Let's take off our costumes," Lane suggested. "We need to be ready to run."

Grey tried to remain calm as she removed her western garb. She joined her team in the tall bushes that lined the building. They hid together in silence, waiting with bated breath. After what felt like forever, Connie finally appeared.

"Hurry!" Connie urged. "Stan and Anne are on the patio. They aren't looking for you yet. If you move fast, they'll never know you were gone."

Grey, Lane, and Blaze bolted through the stairwell. They reached the brown door to their house. Lane stood on his hind legs and pushed the doorknob down. The threesome crept back into their home as quietly as they could. They walked from the front door to the kitchen, and from the kitchen to the living room.

"They're still on the patio," Grey observed.

"What on earth is Stan doing?" Blaze asked.

"He's getting down on his knees," Lane barked. "With a tiny box in his hand."

"He's proposing!" Blaze belted. "What's Anne saying?"

"She said yes!" Lane announced as he leapt in the air.

"We're going to be sisters!" Blaze beamed.

"Family," Lane added.

"Saddle up!" Grey said, grinning. "A change is coming!"

"Look who rode in all striped and sassy now," Lane said, laughing.

"Happy," Grey countered with a full heart. "The word you're looking for is *happy*."

· · · · · · · ·

Grey curled up on her bed. She knew she was lucky. She had everything she'd ever wanted. More importantly, Grey now had everything she ever *needed*.

Like Anne, Grey had needed a family. Grey knew their house would eventually change. Their schedules would gradually shift. The world around them would look different on any given day. They would each race to accomplish whatever needed to be done. But none of that mattered. What mattered were the five of them, sharing in the adventure together.

They had forgotten on which side they'd started. Lane, Blaze, and Grey were now facing the future together.

Grey looked out the window at the blinking lights once more. The mystery had been solved. The lights worked because everyone agreed on their role. Green meant go. Yellow meant pause. Red meant stop. The lights worked together with the passersby. They changed colors to allow everyone an equal chance to proceed.

Grey reflected on her day. Her friends had all worked to achieve a shared goal. Multiple goals, as it had turned out. They were in sync, so they were successful. One animal couldn't have pushed all the buttons. That was never the plan. They had each been given an opportunity to shine.

Maybe life is simple, after all, Grey mused to herself. *Perhaps it's as simple as seeing change as a good thing. With change, we can all move forward. With change, there is light.*

With change,
there is light.

TABLE OF CHARACTERS

Grey, the barn kitten with a magical voice

Lane, the Labrador with magical ears who lives with Grey

Blaze, the Bengal cat who lives with Grey

George, the German Shepherd and chairman of the Argos animal board

Olivia, the Poodle and host of all Argos events

Meg, the Maltese and friend to Blaze

Crown, the Cavalier King Charles Spaniel who helps the Argos animals

Davy, the stray cat and founder of Club David

Rand, the red-eared turtle and friend to Davy

Scout, the Golden Retriever on a mission to search and rescue

The Stars, lighting the way for animals, including—
Polaris "Polly," the North Star
Pherkad "Gamma" and Kochab "Beta," the Guardians
Merak and Dubhe, the Pointers of the Stars
Mizar "Mi" and Alcor "Co," the Doubt Detectors
Alioth "Ali," the Keeper of Joy

ENCORE

On the road to my high-rise
Saw the skyline ahead
Watched the lights blink
From red to green
Found my spot on the bed.

Met a ghost in the hallway
He was waiting for his wife.
Saw the spirit
In her memories
As she joined him in afterlife.

Then a soldier among us
Sat in the stairwell to rest.
Lingering on
Darkened light
Faith fought a staggering test.

Off we raced to Camp David
Determined to find strays.
Crossed the creek
On a magical ride
They'd built a new set of ways.

And now we're learning the ground rules
In the clubhouse of change.
Restoring hope
To those left behind
What a masterful plan they arranged.

So we unpacked our bags
And prepared to head back
Riding fast
On the saddle of friends.
The party of five was on track.

Returned home to our humans
Watched our house become whole.
Found everything
That we need
Tomorrow we'll go for a stroll.

Acknowledging U.S. Veterans

In 1945, my great-grandfather, Mr. William Oscar Irvin, issued the first farm loan in the nation under the G.I. Bill of Rights. The House of Representatives recognized my great-grandfather with this letter and photo. In dedicating *The Land of the Strays* to the military and frontline responders, I have also paid homage to my heritage and continued my family's legacy of honoring U.S. veterans. I am grateful to the men, women, and animals who serve our country. Life always comes full circle.

W.O. IRVIN MAKING THE FIRST FARM LOAN IN THE NATION
TO ROY R. HAYS OF LINDEN TEXAS UNDER THE G.I.
BILL OF RIGHTS

COMMITTEE ON
BANKING AND CURRENCY

SECRETARY:
MRS. LUCILLE SPAIN

Congress of the United States
House of Representatives
Washington, D. C.

April 18, 1945

Mr. A. G. Brown, Deputy Manager
American Bankers Association
22 East 40th Street
New York 16, N. Y.

Dear Mr. Brown:

Enclosed herewith is a newspaper report of the first farm loan made in the Nation under the G. I. Bill of Rights. It was made to Mr. Roy R. Hays, of Linden, Texas, which is in the Congressional District, which I have the honor to represent.

I am well acquainted with Mr. Hays, also Mr. W. O. Irvin, of Daingerfield, Texas, who made the personal loan to Mr. Hays. Mr. Irvin is one of the most progressive, public-spirited, unselfish, generous citizens of East Texas. He took a personal interest in Mr. Hays and will, no doubt, assist other veterans to re-establish themselves upon returning from military service.

Just thought you would be interested in the clipping.

Sincerely yours,

Wright Patman.

269

Acknowledgments

My gratitude to the following—

To Lou, for everything.

To Camille, for your lifelong friendship, humor, and unwillingness to judge others.

To Nancy Harrison, for your genius illustrations and commitment to detail.

To Greenleaf Book Group, for your support in the publishing process.

To George D. Hamilton, for your guidance in honoring the U.S. military and support in making the first donation to the Nilsson Open A Dor Foundation to provide sheltered animals with loving homes. Thank you for continuing to lay the foundation to give back.

To Texas Agriculture Commissioner Sid Miller, an Reb Wayne, Kevin Moomaw, Gary D. Compton, an George D. Hamilton for recognizing the Loodor Tales Series and *The Land of the Strays* in the state of Texas.

To Michael Ziegler, Speedway Motorsports, and George D. Hamilton for spotlighting *The Land of the Strays*.

For more information about Summer Nilsson and the Loodor Tales Series, visit www.loodor.com